EXPOSED

(VIRUS, PART II)

RJ Crayton

CONTENTS

1

Elijah sat on the cold, hard floor, his eyes fixed on Boxcar Willie on the other side of the dimly lit cargo train. Boxcar Willie was such a stupid name. At one time it had been the stage name of a performer who sang about riding the rails. It had come to be the generic name of anyone who rode the rails to get around. Only, there was nothing generic or song-inspiring about this man.

This Boxcar Willie was a savage who wanted Lijah's little sister. The old pervert appeared to be sleeping, his chest rising and falling in a steady rhythm as he lay under a grimy blanket. Lijah didn't trust him. Not enough to close his eyes and leave her unprotected.

He glanced at Elaan for a second. His eyes instinctively returned to the man who'd demanded his sister be his "nighttime companion" for the duration of the ride. They'd nixed that. Only, Willie didn't seem the type to give up easily. But neither did Lijah, and he wouldn't let that man hurt Elaan. His brief glance had shown she was safely asleep, curled up in a ball. She had to be cold. He was shivering himself; the car was freezing. Lijah didn't have a thermometer, but if he had to guess, it was probably somewhere in the fifty degree range. Not freezing, but by no means warm. He glanced at her again. She looked so cold over there.

A wave of guilt washed over him. It was his fault she'd moved away from Josh. They'd be warmer together, but she'd caught a glimpse of Lijah just as she was snuggling up to Josh, and she'd seen it. She'd seen his jealousy, and she'd moved.

God, he was a horrible brother. He'd been telling himself his feelings for Josh had nothing to do with his opposition to the two of them being together, but that had been a lie. He'd been lying to himself so he wouldn't feel bad about keeping them apart. He'd lied to her earlier, when she asked about his feelings. He'd done a reverse guilt trip, turned the tables. "You think that if I had a crush on a guy that my baby sister liked, that I would tell her not to get involved, just so I could feel better?" he'd asked her. "That I would hurt my baby sister's heart just so mine wouldn't?"

And she'd felt the appropriate guilt and backed off. Only it was a lie. He'd done exactly what she'd accused him, and he was a horrible human being for doing so. He was stupid, too, because crushing on a guy who wasn't even gay was an idiotic move.

If they hadn't been locked in quarantine together, he was sure he wouldn't have developed feelings for Josh. But being quarantined together — both of them so alone, so afraid, so unique in their dilemma — had forged a bond between them he hadn't expected. They had been so close, had talked so much. And he got a slight vibe from Josh, or at least he thought he had. Only, the circumstances had clouded his judgment, had turned wishful thinking into his reality. And when he realized that Josh wasn't like him, that Josh was into Elaan, he should've let it go. He didn't. He decided he couldn't bear to see them together, and he concocted a bunch of reasons it was a bad idea. Reasons that made sense to Josh, and almost made sense to him, but deep down, he'd known the truth.

He'd done the first decent thing for the two of them a few hours ago. He closed his eyes for a second and thought back to his conversation with Josh near the river. They'd left Elaan alone in the jeep and gotten far enough to have some privacy, when Josh let loose on him.

"What the hell is this about?" he'd spat, breathing heavily with anger.

They'd been so contentious recently. It hurt that Josh had started to view him with dread, and by then, with contempt. "I wanted to apologize," Lijah said.

Josh took a step back, and stared. "Apologize?"

Lijah nodded, focused on the ground. "I haven't been fair to you and Elaan. Down there, it was different. Down there, it was about keeping our secret and keeping her away from that. About not letting her know just how damaged we'd gotten, how damaged we could be up here, and maybe I was misguided in that, but I just wanted to protect her. She's my little sister."

Josh came closer and put his hand on his shoulder. The feeling of it was like a spark of pleasure shooting through him, yet there was that aftershock of pain. Because Josh just wanted to be his friend. Josh spoke when Lijah finally met his gaze again.

"I know you want to protect her," Josh said. "So do I."

"I know," Lijah said, sliding away from Josh's touch. "That's why I wanted to talk to you now. I want to ask you to stay with Elaan, to protect her, if anything happens to me."

Josh didn't speak, just stared at Lijah. The breeze chilled them, but neither moved to shield themselves against the wind or work up a shiver for warmth. Finally, Josh nodded. "OK."

"Promise," Lijah said. "Promise me you'll do everything to protect her, to keep her safe, to get her safely to our mother."

Josh said clearly, "I promise. I'll do everything in my power to protect her and to get her to your mother."

Lijah inhaled, his spirits lifting. At least he was doing one thing right. Finally. "If there's a chance the three of us might get caught, know that I'll sacrifice myself. You just take Elaan and get her somewhere safe."

Josh shook his head. "Man, that's crazy. We're not in some war movie. There's no reason you'll need to leave us. We won't need to split up. You won't need to make some grand sacrifice."

Lijah laughed. Grand sacrifice. It wasn't a grand sacrifice. If he came in contact with the sick, he'd be just as deadly as Mark Dayton had been. There was no way he'd allow himself to cause anyone the pain of that disease. He'd die before he ever did that to someone. "Fine," he said. "It's not a movie where I make some grand sacrifice." He stood there, swallowed, his body giving an involuntary shiver against the night cold before continuing. "All I can say is that Elaan is one good thing about this world. She's immune and she needs to live. Her DNA needs to keep going. Me, I'm damaged. I'm one contact from being turned into a plague that could kill thousands more people, so if it comes down to her surviving or me, I know where my place is. I know exactly what I'm going to do."

Josh shook his head. "She wouldn't want that."

"I know," he said. "That's why I'm telling you. Because I want you to explain it to her if it happens."

"But it won't happen," Josh said.

"Good, then," Lijah said, not wanting to fight. "It won't happen, but if it does, you'll explain it to her and protect her. You know what they'll do to her if they catch her. Dad didn't tell her everything, but you know, don't you?"

Josh breathed out and put his hand on Lijah's shoulder again. "My dad told me. The cloning wasn't the end. They want breeders. They'd harvest a fair number of eggs, but they want the immunes to bring the children to term. They think that's the best chance of preserving humanity. More immunes. My dad told me they wanted me, but for obvious reasons, he couldn't agree." Josh laughed darkly as Elijah tried to gauge what he was thinking. "Part of me thinks he would've liked for me to be immune, would've liked me to participate, would've liked his family's DNA shaping all of society, shaping the future of our nation and the world."

Lijah reached up and patted Josh's hand resting on his shoulder. He savored the touch silently before stepping away. He had to stop this infatuation, he told himself. It wasn't healthy. "We've all got problems. My mother left and your father, he's helpful, but has issues, too."

Josh raised his eyebrows. "Issues are fine," he said. "I've learned, through all of this, that people are who they are. You have to take the good with the bad, because the person isn't who they are without both pieces. My dad has plenty of traits I don't like, but he has a ton of instincts I respect. His desire to protect me isn't that different from your desire to protect Elaan."

Lijah nodded. Good with the bad. Yeah, he wished he'd discovered Josh's Zen-like state. He couldn't accept the bad that came with his mother or with himself or any other carriers. He couldn't say that out loud, though. Not to Josh. He was like Elaan that way, hopeful. About humanity, about people, about the future. "We should go back or she'll get worried," Lijah said, tipping his head in the direction of the jeep.

Lijah opened his eyes, the memory fading. Boxcar Willie was asleep in his spot. Lijah peeked at Elaan and Josh, both asleep. She shivered and rolled over. He'd been such a jerk. He needed to get himself together. He'd lied to her, but she'd seen right through his lies. She'd seen his hurt and decided not to add to it. Now she was freezing.

He stood and went over to her. She was slumped in a heap facing the opposite direction as Josh, who was snoring. Lijah kneeled and gently tried to reposition her so she was closer to Josh where she'd be warmer. He needed to make sure she was alright. As he nudged her, she stirred. "Shhh," he said softly. "Go back to sleep." When she was younger, she used to want to stay up late to watch movies, but she always fell asleep — and early. Their parents wouldn't fight her, just let her fall asleep on the sofa. Then their father would carry her to bed, and when she'd half wake up, he'd say, "Shhh, go back to sleep." And then she'd be out like a light. Just like that.

"Shhhhh," he said again softly as she turned away

from Josh. But she didn't just roll over. She startled awake, opening her eyes and scanning the room, as if confused about her whereabouts. Her breathing quickened, she tensed, and tried to back away, only to smack into the wall behind her.

"Hey," he said softly, watching as she tried to get her bearings. "It's alright, it's me." He turned behind him to make sure that Elaan wasn't frightened of something behind him, like Willie. Nope. Willie was still in the opposite corner, apparently asleep. Lijah turned back to his sister, who had oriented herself to the surroundings. Her breathing was normal.

"I didn't mean to wake you," he said. "I just thought I could slide you over a bit, the way Mom and Dad did when you were smaller."

She raised an eyebrow, and he was sure she thought he was crazy. Perhaps that was crazy. She wasn't a kid anymore, and moving her had been to allay his guilt as much as it had been to try to help.

"Why were you moving me?"

He avoided her gaze, instead eyeing Josh, who was huddled a little ways over, his mouth humming with a soft snore. Lijah sighed and sat next to his sister, so she was flanked by him and Josh. "You were shivering," he said, pressing his back against the wall of the boxcar. "I thought you'd be warmer if you were lying next to…" He paused before answering, peering directly across the room at Willie, wondering if the man were really asleep. It was better to be safe than sorry. He tipped his head toward Josh and said, "You'd be warmer next to Ethan."

She did a quick double take, but then her sleep-disrupted brain seemed to remember their fake names. "I'm fine."

"No you're not," he said. "That's my fault, and I'm sorry."

"It's not your fault."

Lijah chuckled. "It is." He pulled his knees up to his chest. "Today, or I guess it was really yesterday, you asked if I had another reason for being upset about you and, um, Ethan. I said no. But that wasn't true." He turned and her eyes were kind and understanding. Shame reared in his gut. "What you thought was my motive was true. I didn't realize I was doing it for that reason until you said it, and I hadn't meant to be unfair to you two. So, I'm sorry. He's a good guy, and I'm fine with you two being together."

Elaan nodded, but she didn't quite seem to believe him.

"I saw you lean toward him tonight, but then you saw me and stopped. You seemed to think I was mad, and then you laid down in the opposite direction," he said. "I wasn't mad. I felt bad that I'd mistreated you two. You shouldn't be cold when lying closer to him will keep you warm. I really, truly don't want that for you."

She rested her head on his shoulder. "I'm fine, and I'm not going to make things hard for you if I can help it."

"It's not hard for me," he shot back, with more force than was necessary.

"I know that certain things are personal, but this isn't something you had to hide from us," she said. "We understand. We love you. It doesn't matter to us one way or the other."

He tried not to sigh, refrained from shaking his head. "I know it doesn't matter to you," he finally said.

She didn't say anything for a while, the rattling train and Josh's soft snores the only noises. Finally, she turned to him, a crease in the center of her forehead, and said determinedly, "It doesn't matter to Mom and Dad, either."

He looked at his hands. His nails were dirty. He wondered when they'd gotten that grimy. Perhaps walking through the trees or pushing the jeep into the river. "You think it doesn't matter to them because nothing you did wrong ever mattered to them," Lijah said. "You have always made mistakes and been different, and they have always been OK with that. When you did something different or not quite right, Mom and Dad expected it. They were OK with you. They expected the unexpected. But with me, I fit in. I did exactly what they wanted me to do. And on that rare occasion that I did something they didn't expect or didn't approve of, the disappointment in their eyes was so deep. It was as if I'd cut into their souls with a poisoned dagger. They never saw you that way. They decided that you were going to be different. I was supposed to be dependable and what they wanted."

Elaan touched his arm. "You are exactly what they want," she said.

He smiled. Sometimes she reminded him of their mother. But in a good way. The good memories of Shonda Woodson, when she was kind and compassionate. Elaan was like their mother. Just without the expectations. Elaan had never heard the conversations he'd had with his mother where she expressed her disapproval. Shonda loved him, but she had so many expectations, ones he always strived to fulfill. He wasn't perfect. Not the way his mother had wanted him to be. She'd never expected Elaan to be perfect. He hated the double standard. Elaan's freedom from expectation had caused her to accept people as they were, the way she accepted him right now. "Thanks," he said. "But I'd rather not talk about this right now." He tipped his head toward Josh, who was still asleep. "Please don't tell him. I don't want him to feel uncomfortable."

"Of course," she said. "There's nothing for me to tell." Elaan hunched her shoulders and tilted her head from side to side to stretch out. The cold steel floor of a boxcar didn't make the most comfortable bed.

"You should go back to sleep. You need your rest. I'll keep watch."

She shrugged. "I'm kind of awake now, and I think it will be hard to go back to sleep."

Of course, he thought. Elaan. Expect the unexpected. He'd come over to help make her comfortable, and instead, he'd awakened her.

"Hey," she said, as if she'd just had an epiphany. "What did Dad's letter say?"

The letter. He'd forgotten about it. Everything had happened so fast that he hadn't even looked. "I haven't read it," he said. He crawled over to where he'd been sitting earlier, grabbed the backpack, and then slid back to Elaan. He pulled the letter from the backpack and stared at the envelope.

He wasn't actually sure he wanted to read it. The map had been helpful, but the letter was long. Several handwritten pages. He hadn't been able to see it well in the dark, but he'd read the opening line, "If you're reading this, it means I'm dead." Only, his father had given it to him, now. He was apprehensive to see it again. Afraid to know what his father thought was so important for him to know in the event that he died.

"You gonna open it?" Elaan asked.

He nodded, and pulled the letter out of the envelope.

2

Elaan watched as Lijah opened the letter, wondering what it said. The light from across the room was fairly diffuse, so it wasn't the best for reading. Lijah held the letter close to his face, his eyes moving side to side as he took in their father's words.

She turned away, wanting to give him privacy. Her own backpack was at her feet, and she wondered if her father had written a letter to her, too. She probably should've considered that earlier, but Lijah's letter had contained a map, which made her think that it was instructions on getting to her mother. But Lijah's letter had lots of pages. It wasn't something her father had scrawled out in the moments between finding out they were in danger and heading up to the lab. It had to have been something he'd written earlier. So maybe he'd written one for her, too.

She'd found Lijah's letter accidentally, but she'd been so preoccupied with what the letter could mean and with what Lijah and Josh had gone into the woods to talk about, that she hadn't even thought to go through her pack. She leaned forward and unzipped the bag, her eyes glancing up briefly to make sure Willie was still sleeping. He was. She gave an involuntary shiver. Willie gave her the creeps, especially with what he'd suggested. And that so-called hug. He'd groped her without permission and pressed himself hard against her. Even that small act fully clothed made her feel violated. The thought of what he actually wanted to do to her made her want to vomit. Perhaps that was part of the reason she couldn't go back to sleep. She knew her brother would do all in his power to protect her, but Willie had a gun and there was very little Lijah could do about that. Except get shot. She shuddered. She didn't want anyone hurt.

She pushed from her mind all the things that could go wrong on this trip. Returning her focus to the bag, she pulled out the contents and set them in her lap. At the top of the bag were the jeans and long-sleeved shirt she'd worn before changing into the military fatigues. Beneath that were more clothes, neatly folded: six underpants, two bras, three pairs of wool socks, three long-sleeved shirts, and two pairs of leggings. The leggings had been a strategic decision. They weren't the warmest pants, but they were thin and easy to pack. There was another sweater, a thin black cashmere one. There were also a couple of soft N-95 face masks, the kind people had worn during the outbreak, to keep germs away. She didn't really need one, since she was immune. Maybe it was for show, so she'd seem like other worried people and not stand out. Finally, there was a thin, clear packet a little larger than a four-by-six photograph, with a silvery foil in it. In black print on the plastic, it said "Mylar covering." She didn't know what it was for, but figured it had to serve some use if her father packed it.

And that was it. The complete contents of the pack. Or maybe not. Even though it looked like it should be the bottom of the pack, it wasn't. The smooth nylon fabric matched the rest of the inside of the pack, but it was hard and lumpy beneath the fabric. She squinted into the bag, holding it out toward the light on the other side of the boxcar. She couldn't see much, as the backpack interior was all black. She stuck her hand in and ran her fingers along the edge of the bag, feeling something rough and ridged: a zipper.

A hidden compartment? Or just a second pocket that appeared somewhat hidden in the crappy light. Probably the latter, she thought. She ran her fingers along the edges until she found the zipper's hook and then unzipped the fabric. Folding back the flap, she pulled out what was hidden: a rectangular black nylon pouch that was heavy. It closed like an envelope, the flap held in place by Velcro.

"What is that?" Lijah asked.

She turned to see him staring at her. She'd forgotten he was there. "I don't know," she admitted. "I realized I hadn't checked what was in the pack, and Dad packed it. I thought maybe he'd left me a letter too."

Lijah nodded. "He did." Elaan stared intently, wondering why he sounded so confident. "His letter says he left letters for both of us. That we need both letters, because each one has part of what we need for the trip."

Elaan pulled back the Velcro flap and peered inside. Her mouth opened in surprise but she managed to muffle the gasp. She threw a glance toward Willie to make sure he hadn't awakened and then back to the pouch. Silver and gold coins. They were in plastic containers, as they were collector's pieces, but she knew exactly what they were. Her parents had given her and Lijah each a coin every year for their birthday. Most years were pure silver and worth fifty or sixty bucks a piece, but for years that were multiples of fives, their parents had given them a gold coin. Those were worth more, a lot more. She'd thought each coin had cost around a thousand dollars. She had remembered her parents saying they'd appreciate them when they got older. They'd only seen the gold coins on their birthday, and then their parents had put them in the safe in the house.

Only, they weren't in the safe now. They were here in her bag. Stuck among the coins was a small USB flash drive. The letter G had been written on it with a Sharpie. Clearly it was meant for her, because her middle name was Grace. Because she and Elijah had the same first initial, her parents labeled all their stuff by their middle initials. Her things were G and his were J, for Jacob.

Also inside the pouch was the thing she had wanted to begin with: an envelope with her name on it. She pulled the envelope out and handed Lijah the nylon pouch. She thought he'd seen what was inside, but she wanted to make sure. He took the bag from her but didn't say anything. She eyed the letter in her hand and wondered what it said. Even though she'd wanted this letter, a wave of apprehension hit. Curiosity about what it said percolated in her brain. Yet overwhelming dread simmered there, too, especially since Lijah hadn't told her what his letter said. She wondered if the contents of the letter could somehow make their situation worse.

"Open your letter," Lijah said.

She slid her fingers along the outside of the

smooth white envelope but made no attempts to open it. Lijah's insistence that she read it was making her more nervous about its contents. "What'd yours say?" she asked, laying the envelope down on the pile of clothes in her lap.

Lijah made sure Willie was still in his corner. "Read yours, and then we can swap," he said.

Unable to hide her confusion, her eyebrows squished together. At home, Lijah was a complete "don't touch my stuff" kinda guy. The idea that he'd just hand over his letter was as bizarre as a destitute Bill Gates. "You'll let me see yours?"

He nodded. "Read yours," he said. "You'll see."

Her brow creased at his refusal to speak, at his insistence that she see for herself. What was so bad that the words couldn't be spoken, even in brevity, on a boxcar chugging through the darkness toward St. Louis? The knot in her stomach tightened, yet her curiosity had gained the upper hand. She took a deep breath, her hands trembling from the bumpy ride, opened the envelope, and pulled out her letter.

Elaan,

If you're reading this, it means the worst has happened; I've died. It saddens me to think that I've seen you through such a short part of your life. I was lucky enough to keep my mother through her sixties, and into my thirties, though you never met her. I got to keep my father another twenty years, and you, of course, met him. Still, losing them was hard, and I was an adult.

Losing both your parents at seventeen seems unduly cruel. However, I know the world we live in now is one of cruelty, danger, and disease. Part of that is my fault. I should have been an "alarmist" with the rest of them. I took comfort in science and logic. Then God laughed at me and said, "Let me remind you that science is all about discovery. Here is something new for you to discover."

I'm writing this two days after we moved to the scientist housing. I keep it in a locked box inside my room. That is just enough security to keep it safe from prying eyes, but loose enough to allow you to retrieve it when the time comes. I know Lijah knows what to do, but you, my sweet Laani, are in the dark.

So, let me start at the beginning. A few months ago, I learned that Mark Dayton, the man who started this awful pandemic, was not an only child, as we believed. His mother gave birth to a daughter, whom she gave up for adoption shortly afterward. She didn't tell her family, and Mark barely remembered it because he was only three at the time and his mother never spoke of it. He'd almost thought it a figment of his imagination. That is until his mother died two weeks before his scheduled missionary trip to South America. He held the funeral and also had the task of clearing out her personal belongings. He found a document with the baby's footprint and adoption papers. He hired a private eye to find his sister, asked his aunt to wrap up the remainder of his mother's estate, and went on his trip.

As you know, he returned a month later and began unknowingly infecting people. Among the first people he saw was the detective. The private eye had found his sister: Shonda Woodson.

I'm sure that news is a shock to you. It was a shock to

me, as well. Dayton was glad the detective had found his sister, and he wanted to see her. But, this was new to him, and he wasn't sure how to proceed. So he decided to find out all he could about her before introducing himself. He read through the detective's file, but also Googled her to learn what the Internet could tell him about her. There was a decent amount of information to go through, so he busied himself with that, as well as getting reacquainted with his life.

A week after he returned from South America, he'd decided to call his newly found sister. But before he got a chance, he received a call from the CDC. The first case of the Helnoan virus had been detected in this country. A man on the flight he'd taken from South America was sick. Medical officials told him it was unlikely he was sick, but asked him to watch for symptoms and go to a doctor immediately if he experienced them.

We know now, he never had any symptoms and never would. But he didn't know that, and decided he wasn't going to try to find his sister until the mandatory three-week incubation period had passed. The CDC nurse told him that many people got sick before the three weeks, but that he should wait the full period, just in case. He tried to stay fairly secluded, but he'd already spent two weeks ministering to his congregation.

Then two members of his church became sick. It was odd since they hadn't left the country. Why were they sick? He had a sinking feeling that he might be at the root of it, but how could he be? He had no symptoms.

He took the file the detective had given him and put it in his bank's safe deposit box. He didn't know why he wanted to lock away this information, but he did. Another church member became ill, and that's when he turned himself in to the CDC for testing. We know what it showed. Only it was too late to stop things. The epidemic had begun already.

Before we were sent underground, the government decided Mark was too dangerous to live. Mark asked to see me. He told me that he knew they were going to kill him. I don't know how he knew. When I asked, he simply pointed to the heavens. I was never much a man of God. That was more your mother's dominion. He told me that his safe deposit box had information in it, information about his sister who'd been given up for adoption. His sister's name, he told me in a whisper, was Shonda. He said she'd had been adopted by a Missouri family. I thought he was trying to rile me, trying to do something nefarious. Though, I could not figure out, for the life of me, what that nefarious thing was. There was no advantage to lying to me. It was what he said next that chilled me, and roused me to action. Those are the words I will never forget: "If she's like me, protect her. Promise me you'll protect her."

His eyes were wide with sorrow, grief, fear, and even, dare I say it, mercy. Mercy for me because I had decided his fate and hers, too. "Promise me," he begged again.

I nodded and left. I just knew he was wrong. It couldn't be her. It couldn't be. But I went to a pay phone. Do you know how hard it is to find a pay phone? No one uses them anymore, but I found one in a rundown neighborhood, and I called your mother. I told her what I was worried about. She drew two samples of blood and had DeeDee bring them to me at the lab. When I tested them, when I found out that the blood behaved very similar to Dayton's — it had a symbiotic relationship with the virus — I was devastated. I told her she had to leave, and she had to stay away from people.

We created a plan and she left.

I can't tell you where she went. Lijah knows. You'll need his help to find her. I feared putting too much information in one letter, lest someone find one and use it to try to hurt her. But I also wanted you to know. You are not all alone in this world. Even though I am gone, you still have your mother. And you can see her. Your immunity means she poses no harm to you. In fact, she can be a comfort and help to you.

When you leave the scientist housing, when the pandemics are over, go and find her, so that you are not alone.

The last thing you need to know is that I've put you and your brother's coins in your bag in case you need them. Yes, there are banks and we have money in our accounts, but it's not clear how easy it will be to access all of those things once the disease has run its course. I've heard already that people have panicked and tried to pull money out of banks, and the government has stopped multiple withdrawals. Some people only want silver and gold. Luckily, you and Lijah have some. You each have three gold coins. But Lijah has sixteen silver and you only have fourteen. I thought your mother was silly for giving silver and gold coins as a gift, but it was something her parents had done for her as a child and she cherished those coins. She took hers with her when she left.

After Dayton died, I offered to help the government settle his estate. I closed his safe deposit box and burned the file on your mother. The only evidence that he had a sister is in this letter and now in your and Lijah's heads. Burn the first pages of this letter. I know sometimes we find sentimental value in holding on to things, but nothing but danger for you or your mother can come from this. I've created one additional page that you can keep forever as a memento. But not these pages.

Dad

p.s. You and Lijah need to work together. Tell him F3, N11; Crystal Circle

The letter ended in the middle of the sheet. Burn it, he'd said. Only keep the last page. Her fingers glided over the cursive. She pictured her father's hands laboring over the paper as he wrote down the dangerous truth. She sighed, and shook her head. It was all too much. Her father wasn't dead, as he'd thought he'd be, but he was gone from her life for the moment. The reality of that started to hit home. She took a deep breath to steady her mind and calm herself. She didn't want to be overwhelmed by the feelings of loss the letter had dragged to the surface. There's more to the letter, she told herself, as she moved the top sheet of paper to find the single page her father suggested she keep.

"Courage isn't having the strength to go on — it is

going on when you don't have strength."
-*Napoleon Bonaparte*

You have courage and strength. Go on, my love. Know that you have brought me more joy than you can ever know. I will love you for all of eternity. When things seem grim, think of me and know I will be watching over you on your journey. Think of me when you need to be reminded that you still have strength. All my love,

Dad.

A tear trickled down Elaan's cheek. She sighed. She missed him already. Even though he wasn't dead, he'd given her this letter and these coins so they could make it to her mother.

Lijah put a hand on her shoulder. "You alright?"

"Yeah," she mumbled as she wiped away the tear. "Let's swap." She handed him the first sheets of her letter, opting to keep the last for herself.

Lijah handed her his letter, but he didn't appear to keep anything back. A twinge of guilt emerged, and Elaan wondered if she was being selfish for not sharing the same way Lijah had.

She started to read Lijah's letter.

Elijah,

If you're reading this, it means I'm dead.

I'm so sorry that I'm not there for you now, in what must be a difficult time. There is so much I wanted to say to you while I was alive, and if you're reading this, it means I've died without saying it. You are a brilliant and strong young man, stronger than I ever have been or could hope to be. Even though I know you'll cringe when I say this, you get your strength from your mother. She has a force of will that most human beings have never encountered, let alone had burst forth from their own bodies. I think you are much the same, only this world being how it is has caused you to doubt yourself. Don't. You are very capable and very strong.

I know you think that what's happened to you is a curse. And I can't say that I blame you for thinking it. Receiving a vaccine that didn't do what it was supposed to do is awful. I apologize for not being there to direct you, to help you understand the ramifications of what could happen. Though, truth be told, neither Kingston nor myself had any inclination the side effects would be as dramatic.

Still, I do not want you to be despondent or think things are over for you. We are men of science, and we know that every problem has a solution, even if we are unable to think of it immediately. Your solution is there. I feel it in my bones. Kingston and I have been working on it, and you've been, too. You know there are possibilities, if only we can illuminate the right ones. Part of me hopes I'll find this note a year from now (which is just after we've entered the SPU), look at it, and laugh because we've come up with a solution.

But if we haven't solved this problem, know that you can continue the research. You and your mother. You have everything you need at your fingertips. You just need a safe location to work things out. I've provided you a map of a place you can go. You and your sister must work together though. She's immune to the virus, and you're both young, so I think you'll stand a better chance in the post-virus world if you are together. She has something you need. And you have something she needs. Together, you make a whole. Our whole family for the moment. Take your sister and go to your mother.

I know you worry about her condition. Please don't. Hah. Easier said than done, right? Yes, she's a carrier, but she is only a carrier of the heavy particulate strain. This is a good thing. It means she's unlikely to contaminate anyone, especially you. Her status may even be a good thing. I've sometimes wondered if her strange situation — immune to the airborne strain, but carrier of the fluid-passed strain — somehow holds the key to engineering a vaccine that actually works. You should talk to her. She's a good person who loves you very much.

I love you with all my heart, and I'm proud of you. Please take care of your sister. And destroy this letter after you've finished reading it. All except the last page. That you may keep, if you're feeling sentimental, but sometimes I think Elaan and I are the only sentimental ones in this family. You and your mother are practical, and that is, as much as I used to tease your mother for it, a very important trait to have.

-Dad.

P.S. 4801. Your sister has the rest.

The next page said only one line.

I am, and always have been, proud of you. I love you. Stay strong.
   -Dad.

Elaan handed her brother his letter, and he did the same in return.

"So, he thinks it can be fixed," Elaan said, trying to be cryptic in case Boxcar Willie could hear. Yet, she could barely hear herself over the din of the train, so she was pretty sure Willie couldn't hear her all the way across the boxcar.

Lijah shrugged. "It doesn't matter," he said.

"How can you say that?" she asked. "It's the only thing that matters now. And she can help you. You can't hate her now. Not if she can help."

Lijah shook his head. "I don't hate her," he said, his antipathy making it hard for Elaan to believe him. "My feelings toward her are complicated, but that's not the important part. What's important is that help will be good. Feeling warm and fuzzy toward the source of the help is just a bonus you have and I don't."

She wondered how he could still be so hostile. She wanted to ask him more, but decided this wasn't the time or the place. She took the letter that had all the details and ripped it in half. "Do you have a match?"

"We can't do that here," Lijah replied. "Just give it to me, and I'll take care of it once we get off in Terra Haute."

Terra Haute. That wasn't their destination. In fact it was pretty far from Dahinda, she thought. But she still couldn't quite visualize both cities in relation to one another. "Can I see the map?" she said.

Lijah nodded, pulled out the map, and handed it to her. As she unfolded it she realized it was a pretty big sheet of paper, probably eleven by seventeen inches. When Lijah had said it was an Illinois map, she thought it had just Illinois on it, but it also included Missouri, Iowa, and Wisconsin. The edges of Indiana and Kentucky appeared as well. If all someone had was that map, there was no way they'd be able to figure out where Lijah and Elaan were headed. A six-state radius was big. On the map, she found Terra Haute marked by a large dot.

Unfortunately, a search for Dahinda yielded nothing. A creep of panic. "Where is it? Where's the dot for —" she wanted to say Dahinda aloud, but finished with "the place were going."

Lijah chuckled. "Didn't you read your letter?"

She wasn't sure what he meant. Then it hit her: F3, N11. "Oh," she said, as she used her pointer finger to locate the spot on the map. There wasn't a town name, but that must be Dahinda. It was right next to the Spoon River. She'd heard of the river but couldn't remember where or why.

It was a pretty long way from Terra Haute to the F3, N11. "Do you think we should try to renegotiate, given what we've found?"

Lijah shook his head. "No, it's better we just get off where we said. We knew we were going to have to travel some of the way on our own. It's best he doesn't know where we're headed."

She nodded, folded the map, and held it out to Lijah. He hesitated before taking it and opening it up. "I'm not eidetic like Josh, but I'll do my best to memorize this, and then you can keep it."

Her eyebrows squished together in consternation.

"Eidetic?"

Lijah gave her a look that made her feel like she should've known, but then he softened and said, "It's the official term for having a photographic memory."

She wondered if he was joking, but she could think of no reason to joke about that.

"He's never mentioned it to you?" Lijah asked.

She shook her head and could've sworn she saw the ghost of a smile on his face at knowing something about Josh that she didn't. "It never came up."

Lijah nodded. "Yeah, I think he's a little self-conscious about telling people," he admitted. "But he said he had it earlier, so if I get separated from the two of you, he'll know where to go. And if for some reason all three of us get separated — and there's no reason we should — then I want you to keep it. I'm pretty sure if I study all the routes, I'll be able to get there. Just remember the address."

"What address?"

"Crystal Circle," he whispered. "I had the 4801, the street number; you had the street name."

"Oh," she said, as it dawned on her what her father had done. There was a bit of folly in her father's plan. If she and Lijah had been separated, their letters would have been worthless. It had all worked out in the end, but she found it odd that he'd leave so much to chance.

Elaan glanced at Lijah as he stared at the map. Then she turned to Willie. His chest rose and fell steadily. She wondered if she shouldn't be trying to sleep, too. It was already late. Breathing out, her eyes found Lijah again. He planned to stay awake to keep her safe. "If you want, I can study it, and then you can hold on to it."

He laughed. "You know, you can't even give people directions to the house until you get within a two-mile radius. I think you're best keeping it."

She scowled. "I'm very good with maps, when I need to be," she said. "Besides, I should study it anyway, in case it gets lost." The torn halves of the letter her father had written were in his lap. "The last page of Dad's letter was only half full. Why don't you take the scraps and trace part of the map, too?"

His mouth parted slightly, as if he didn't believe she'd had a good idea. Then he shrugged. "Why don't you get some sleep, sis? We have a long day tomorrow."

For once, she agreed with him. She was tired, and even more drained after reading her father's words. She tucked the part of the letter she was saving into her backpack and made sure the coin bag was secure. She said to Lijah, "Should I give you your stuff?" She dipped her head toward the bag of coins. "In case we get separated."

He stole another glance at Willie. "I want to let things settle a bit before we do that," he said. "Just get some sleep."

Elaan nodded. She repacked her clothes, settled the backpack next to her like a pillow, laid her head on it, and shut her eyes.

3

Lijah could barely keep his eyes open. He glanced at his watch: 4 a.m. He wasn't sure if the watch was a saving grace or part of the torture of the trip. Without the watch, it was impossible to tell how much time had passed on the train, which was one monotonous, loud, creaky ride. Willie was fairly still over there, but Lijah supposed the man would have to wake soon. There had to be another checkpoint coming up. He couldn't imagine traveling much longer without one.

Though, he'd never done this before, so he could be totally wrong. In any event, he needed to wake Josh, so he could take over. A pang of jealousy washed over him as he saw that Elaan and Josh had managed to gravitate toward each other as they slept. Despite the noise, the cold, and the grime, they'd managed to lean into each other and seem at ease.

He wished he could get Josh out of his head. It wasn't right. He took a deep breath and crawled over to Josh. Tapping him on the shoulder, he said, "Wake up." Josh didn't move. Lijah grasped his shoulder and shook him slightly. "Wake up," he said a little louder, hoping to rouse Josh but not disturb his sister. Josh opened his eyes, groggily at first, but then widened his eyes and stiffened as he took in his surroundings.

"It's OK," Lijah said. "It's me. You're fine, Ethan.

You're on the train here with me and my sister, Priya."

Josh stared at Lijah a minute, squinting as if trying to wrap his mind around what was being said. And then, his face relaxed, and he nodded. "Yes, Daanish," Josh said. "I remember. It just took me a minute."

"I need to get some sleep," he said. "Can you keep an eye on her?" He tipped his head toward Elaan, then back toward Willie.

Josh nodded. "Absolutely."

Lijah went back to his spot in the corner and closed his eyes. A moment later, though, a hand rested on his shoulder. He opened his eyes. It was Josh. "What?"

"I know you need sleep, and I'm sorry. I'll let you sleep in a minute, but since she's, um, asleep, I just wanted to ask you something."

Lijah nodded, and Josh sat down, facing him, leaving a decent amount of space between them. Part of Lijah wished he'd move closer, while the rest of him knew it was stupid. He needed to stop this, he told himself.

"I know the map, and I remember the best route to get there," Josh said. "But, I'm a little concerned about your —" he stopped abruptly, glanced back at Willie, then scooted slightly closer to Lijah. "I'm concerned about the woman we're going to see. Do you think he was right about her, that she can't cause us problems?"

Lijah rubbed his temples. He was so tired and really not in the mood to discuss his mother, especially with Josh. "Listen, I think he's right," he said firmly. "You know as well as I do that the difference in communicability between the two strains is huge. He saw her bloodwork. I never did. If he says it's not the airborne strain, then I believe him. Besides, he wouldn't lie to us about this. The consequences are too severe."

Josh nodded, as if trying to reassure Lijah that he understood and believed, but Josh's face showed no signs of being assured. His eyes were a little too wide and his mouth downturned. It reminded Lijah of the way Josh had been when they were together in their supposed quarantine. The way he looked after they'd learned the side effects of the vaccine, learned that their lives had just been unalterably changed for the worse, rather than the better.

Lijah reached out and patted his shoulder. "Seriously, it will be alright, man. We'll be fine going there."

Josh half smiled. "You know me too well," he admitted and sighed. "But, I know you, too. I know that even though you asked me to protect your sister." He hesitated, as if grasping for a thought. "And I will. One hundred percent, but I also feel like you're still not OK with it."

Josh turned his head toward Willie. Lijah followed with his eyes, to see if the old man had stirred. He was in the same position, chest heaving up and down with snores, his body rattling slightly in line with the boxcar's tremors.

"I'll stay with her and help her get where we're going," Josh said. "But if things go south, I won't put her in danger. I'll give up to throw them off her scent, no matter what." He leaned in closer to Lijah. "If they want to take us to Facility One, then I can't blame them. We both know the dangers that carriers present. But if it seems like they're coming after me, I'll make sure Elaan gets far away before they catch up. I know you worry about her being with me, but I'm not selfish, Lijah. I won't do anything to put her in danger."

Lijah nodded. "I know, man. I trust you."

Josh smiled and walked back over to Elaan, keeping his eyes trained on Willie the entire time. Josh was a good guy, and Lijah knew that he'd been a jerk to push them apart. Though Josh had bought all his lies — hook, line, and sinker. Josh truly believed that Lijah hadn't wanted Elaan to be with him because he could be a carrier, because the government could come after him and hurt Elaan in the process. That Elaan would be hurt if the government exterminated Josh at Facility One, or made him live in quarantine. And while the reasons he'd given Josh for not being with Elaan were rooted in some truth, they weren't the real reason. Lijah cursed himself for his stupidity and selfishness once more. He vowed to finally do the right thing. With that, he closed his eyes and was asleep in seconds.

4

The slowing of the train roused Elaan from her slumber. Despite the noise, the vibration of the rail car, and its rusty smell, she'd slept soundly. She wasn't quite ready to get up yet, so she sat there with her eyes closed, trying to rest.

She'd been exhausted when she finally closed her eyes last night — or it was technically earlier this morning. The day before had been completely draining. Everything she'd thought she knew was a lie. Her mother wasn't dead. Her mother was alive but in hiding because she was a carrier. The government wanted to experiment on Elaan. And her brother and the guy she hoped would be her boyfriend could become carriers if they came into contact with the disease. It was too much for her brain to digest.

She startled at the odd movement next to her and opened her eyes in time to see Josh get up. Movement in her periphery caused her to turn in time to see Willie striding toward them. She pulled her knees to her chest and tried to back up, but her back was already against the boxcar wall. There was nowhere she could go.

"Ethan," Willie said. It took Elaan a moment to realize he was talking to Josh. The old man smiled down at her through his grizzled beard. "Priya, darlin'."

Elaan nodded, though didn't smile. Before the world went haywire with disease, she'd never been leered at. But having it happen now, she was particularly threatened by it. In the world before, there were laws and police. People couldn't simply grab you off the street and do what they wanted to you. Here, the laws seemed nebulous at best, and Willie clearly paid people to look the other way. He could simply shoot Josh and Lijah and do whatever he wanted to Elaan, and that terrified her.

"She's just waking up," Josh said. "And she could actually use a couple hours more of shut eye. Tell me what you want, and I'll pass it on."

Willie shrugged. "We have another checkpoint," he said. "It's not like the one a couple of hours ago at five a.m. That was a bumblefuck city. They have a checkpoint just to keep up appearances, pretend they're doing something. This is a real checkpoint. They do a car search."

"A car search," Josh said. "What does that mean?"

"It means they're supposed to search each car, making sure it's got only the cargo listed in the manifest. It takes longer and slows everything down. Usually about forty minutes. It's imperative that you stay quiet."

Josh nodded.

"I have a guy who'll come in and inspect the car. I'll pay him his cut and he'll mark us clean. However, there is an inspection overseer, and if he sees or hears anything out of the ordinary, he can do a check himself. He may or may not be open to bribery. Either way, we don't want him on this train, so keep it quiet. Got it?"

Josh nodded. "Yes. Got it."

5

Lijah had only gotten a couple of hours of sleep, and he wasn't that happy to be awakened, even though he figured it must be important. He knew Josh and Elaan wouldn't wake him for no reason, so he refrained from grimacing when he opened his eyes to see Josh squatting in front of him.

"Checkpoint is coming up," Josh said without fanfare. "Willie says a guy may come on board. We need to be quiet. This guy is on the payroll, but his boss is not. We need to make sure we don't give the boss a reason to come aboard."

Lijah nodded. Willie was full of a crap-ton of problems. Lijah wished he hadn't suggested the train. Yes, they were further now than they would've gotten by car, but it could all go to hell any minute. Willie could double-cross them on a whim or because he was a jerk or for any other reason under the sun. And, if something legitimately went wrong — like the checkpoint went bad — Willie would turn them in without a second thought.

Elaan was standing a couple of paces away, leaning on the wall of the boxcar. Josh stood to join her. Lijah thought he could afford to rest for a minute or two more. He was exhausted. Not just physically, but mentally. He'd promised to take Elaan to their mother, but he still wasn't keen on seeing her. He also wasn't keen on spending the trip watching Elaan and Josh hold hands, either.

He wanted a break. He'd been on the run for less than a day, and already he wanted out. He was so pathetic. It was his job to be the strong one, to keep everyone together, to protect them, to get them where they were going. But he was too tired to do it. Too tired to think. He needed to figure out a contingency plan to deal with Willie. He couldn't be trusted, and they'd told him too much about their trip. Yes, St. Louis was a bit of a red herring, but if he decided to tell someone about them, they were screwed.

The train was slowing down, making a loud, squeaky racket as it went over the tracks. He called Elaan by her fake name. She ignored him, either having not heard or forgotten she needed to answer to Priya. He pushed himself off the grimy, mud-caked floor and wiped his hands on his pants. His body felt stiff from several hours curled up on the hard floor.

Elaan turned to him and smiled. He inclined his head, signaling her to come closer. Concern washed over her face, and she took the few steps to him. He leaned in and whispered in her ear. "I'm worried about the train stops. We may need to make a run for it at some point. We may even need to split up. I think we should try to discreetly split the coins. Three ways."

Elaan frowned slightly, but then nodded. She turned, looked at Willie, and then back at Lijah. "I think he'll be distracted getting ready for the checkpoint, so it seems like the best time."

Lijah nodded, and added, "Explain to Josh." He sat down and closed his eyes. He wasn't going to go back to sleep, but he needed to tune things out for a moment. He needed some peace.

Neither Josh nor Elaan spoke to him as the train lumbered toward the checkpoint. Lijah had slept through the previous checkpoints, so he wasn't sure if it was a train station or the middle of nowhere. Because the boxcar was a completely metal box, they couldn't peek out to see what was coming.

Lijah opened his eyes. He stood and watched as Willie loped toward them. The older man's mouth was a stern line when he reached the three of them and said, "The train will stop in less than five minutes. Stay in this corner and don't say anything," Willie said. "Understand?" They all nodded.

Willie walked over to the boxcar door and stood sentry as the train slowed. There was still a decent amount of rattling, so Willie wouldn't hear what they were doing. Lijah motioned to Elaan and Josh for their backpacks. They both handed him their bags. He set them all on the floor against the wall, and Elaan and Josh turned back to face Willie and block Lijah from his view.

Lijah needed to split their monetary supplies so they all had enough, should they get separated. He decided to start with Josh's bag, which held the cash. Josh said he had fifty thousand dollars. Lijah quickly calculated that an even split would have been about $16,600 apiece, but there was no way he could get that precise with Willie just across the train. He opened the bag but didn't know where the money was. He suspected it was the same place it had been in Elaan's bag, the lower zipper pouch. While the cash was his priority, he found himself curious what Josh had packed. Shuffling through the bag, he noted pants, shirts, underwear, a razor, some food, a hard plastic box that had something inside it, but Lijah didn't think it was the money, so he didn't open it. Probably more gadgetry from his father. He stumbled across a handful of condoms and sighed, remembering Kingston shoving them in the bag in front of him and his dad, when Josh had gone over to talk to Elaan in the lab. Kingston was such a jerk. He'd wanted James to cringe at the prospect of his daughter having an orgy and rethink suggesting they go together. But Kingston had no idea how much was on the line for the Woodson family, and a minor orgy was not going to be enough to get James Woodson to suggest Elaan and Lijah go without Josh.

Lijah reached further down, located the lower pouch, and unzipped it. He reached inside and found five distinct stacks of money separated by rubber bands. That probably meant ten thousand in each. He could try to approximate and pull half from one, or simply undercount himself. He'd be alright with less if they got separated. Especially if Willie was right, and people valued bills less than silver and gold. He shoved two stacks in Elaan's bag.

He went into Elaan's bag and found the coin pouch. Quietly, he separated the coins into three mostly even stacks. He again undercounted himself on the silver coins, and then transferred each of the even stacks to Josh's and Elaan's bags and the smaller one to his own. Lijah zipped the three packs and stood. They were all even at this point. Or at least as even as they were going to get.

Lijah tapped Elaan's leg. She turned back, and he gave a simple nod as the train squeaked to a stop, everyone jolting as it did. Willie put a finger to his lips and they stood there, waiting. The waiting seemed to be the worst part. Lijah glimpsed the watch on his wrist. It was ten o'clock.

The idea of standing had seemed good. He thought maybe he could stretch or twist or move about a bit, and still be quiet. But the longer they stood, the antsier he got. He wanted to run or tap his foot. Something, anything at all. Only that seemed like it would make noise. Willie stood unmoving in the doorway.

Lijah checked his watch again. It was ten thirty. A half an hour had passed. He heard the warble of the train doors in nearby cars opening and closing as muffled voices edged closer. Finally, their door clambered open, and Lijah, Elaan, and Josh stepped backward, pressing their backs into the wall.

A tall, thin man in a military uniform stepped onto the boxcar. Willie and the man exchanged glances and some private signals. Then, Willie closed the door of the car and looked to his right, where Lijah, Josh, and Elaan were standing. The military man pointed at them.

"Passengers," Willie said softly, the sound reverberating in the train car.

Lijah lowered his eyes to the ground, not wanting the military guy to think that he was trying to listen in or, worse, memorize his face.

"You're fine," he said. "The chief just got called away. I'm to clear the remainder of the train."

Lijah breathed out in relief and imagined Willie doing the same. The chief, according to Josh, had been the main problem.

"For you," he heard Willie say. He couldn't resist peeking and glimpsed Willie handing the man a pouch.

The man opened the pouch and scanned its contents. He nodded and handed Willie a piece of paper. "There's a change in the schedule at Effingham," he said. "It's explained here."

Willie nodded at the man. Lijah lowered his head, afraid the man would catch him.

He heard the boxcar door slide open again, and the military man said, "All clear here." Lijah looked up as the door closed. Willie had his fingers to his lips, reminding them to keep quiet. Lijah supposed they weren't done yet. There were probably a few more boxcars left to be searched by Willie's guy. They waited about ten more minutes, and then the train started again.

Willie said, "Alright, that's the last big checkpoint prior to Terra Haute. Two more little ones, and then you guys are off."

Lijah nodded. Willie made it seem simple, but Lijah had a feeling it wouldn't be. Lijah was one hundred percent certain that nothing with Willie was ever simple.

6

After the checkpoint, the ride had been fairly uneventful, as far as Elaan was concerned. They'd dug into their food supply, eating a snack. Willie had given them jars to take care of their business, but if Elaan could have held it, she would have. The only good thing was Willie gave them each their own fresh jar. By fresh, she meant apparently unused recently. They appeared to be old mayonnaise jars and smelled of bleach. But you had to do what you had to do.

They were almost at Terra Haute, which meant they were almost through with Willie. Elaan was so glad to be done with him. He was a creepball beyond creepballs. Even now, she could feel his eyes on her, watching her as she sat on the boxcar floor between a sleeping Lijah and an awake Josh. Willie smiled at her, the gap in his teeth menacing her. She kept her head down, staring at her feet, then at the watch on her wrist. It was four forty-five. Willie said they'd get to Terra Haute by five, so it couldn't be that far now. She took a peek and Willie was now busy looking inside his boxes.

She leaned over and whispered in Josh's ear. "Not much longer," she said. "I can't wait to get away from this guy."

Josh whispered back. "Me neither. Just stick close

to us getting off the train. We'll have you go first."

Elaan nodded. First. She wasn't even sure what she would do when she got off. Where would she go? How did the drop-off even work? Weren't there guards? This was a checkpoint, right?

Willie shoved a lid on the box he'd been rummaging in and started walking toward them. Josh stood. Elaan remained seated but nudged Lijah with her elbow. She didn't begrudge him the sleep. He'd been up early the previous day, doing God knows what with Kingston in the lab. He'd stayed awake practically all night to keep her safe from Willie, so she understood why he was exhausted. But now they all had to be on alert because getting off this train wasn't going to be easy. Lijah stirred, and she said loudly, "Daanish, it's your sister, Priya. Wake up."

Lijah opened his eyes reluctantly, and then nodded.

"We're going to stop in a minute," she said.

Lijah glanced at Willie standing in front of them, and he stood. The three men towered over Elaan, overshadowing her until she stood too. Willie smiled at this. Josh's hand brushed against hers gently and he gave her a solid look of support. She took a breath to steady herself. They were almost done. Willie molesting her with his eyes was only going to last a few more minutes, and then they'd be gone.

"So, Terra Haute's a good place to get off," Willie said. "We stop near a cemetery. The military like to joke, 'if we find a stowaway, there's nothing to do but shoot 'em.'"

Easily shot and discarded. That seemed like a very bad place to get off.

"Why exactly is that a good place to get off?" Lijah

asked, mirroring Elaan's thoughts.

"There's a mausoleum at the cemetery not far from the tracks. I generally suggest people get off the train and dart straight into the mausoleum," Willie said. He smiled at her and added, "A mausoleum is an above ground building where you can bury bodies or deposit ashes. They're popular in areas below sea level because flooding can cause the bodies to dislodge. They're also nice for people who don't like the idea of being buried. My mother wanted a mausoleum." His eyes got wistful for a moment, as if some memory of his mother had overtaken him. "We couldn't even get anyone to come get the body, people were so scared." He sighed and shook off his sentiment. "Anyway, this mausoleum is good for you guys because it's less than twenty yards from the track and once you get inside, you can't be seen. Wait there until the train leaves, then you can find shelter nearby for the overnight."

"OK," Lijah said. "So how do we get off the train?"

"The inspector is going to come on to inspect the train for contraband and mark it clear. I'm going to tell him I have three passengers that need off." He pointed to the doors on either side of the car. "You can unload cargo from either side," Willie said. "Our inspector will come in through this door." He pointed at the door to his right. "He'll open the other door, the cemetery side, while on the train. Once he clears the car, we wait two minutes, then you get off the train and get to the mausoleum. Go quickly and quietly. The inspector won't say anything, and no one else should be watching. The two minutes allows him to get his second inspector to go on the next car. But you have to hurry, because if the other guy, who isn't on the payroll, sees you, you could end up captured. If they don't shoot you and leave you for dead, they'll take you into custody and drop you in the checkpoint holding cell they use for stowaways."

Elaan didn't like the sound of that. It was iffy and problematic. But she supposed it was the best they were going to get.

Lijah nodded, so she followed suit. Willie smiled at them and said, "Gather your things and stand in this corner, ready to go. I'll wave you over when it's time to get off." The train began to slow. "Be quiet the entire time. OK?"

They nodded again and watched Willie go stand near door as they put their backpacks on. The waiting was long and tedious, even though it was really only a minute or two. Elaan stood, unmoving, even though she felt like jogging a few laps, or sprinting as fast as she could away from the train. She just wanted off.

The train squeaked to a stop and the three of them waited. After a couple more interminable minutes, the boxcar door slid open and a short, stocky man in a military uniform stepped in and closed the door.

Willie greeted the man with a soft spoken, "I have passengers exiting here."

The man looked over at them, nodded, and turned back to Willie. "Open the door and wait two minutes," he said. "I'll get my second to inspect car three. That's regular cargo, yes?"

Willie nodded. The military man turned to them. "Wait exactly two minutes, then exit this door. You'll have an additional minute to get out of sight before the train starts moving again."

They nodded, and the inspector left. Willie walked across to the other door and stood until the inspector signaled, then they both opened their doors. Willie's went only about two feet wide, while the inspector's went all the way. The inspector jumped off the car and closed the door.

Willie motioned them over. Josh arrived at the door's edge first, Elaan behind him, and Lijah pulling up the rear. Josh, pensive for a moment, glanced at Willie and then stepped away from the door and motioned for Elaan to go first. She didn't want to be first off, but she also didn't like the way Willie leered, so she swallowed and nodded at Josh. It was probably best for her to go first. She took a step forward, ready to get off the train, but Willie held up his hand. He was wearing a watch and seemed to be counting the seconds as they ticked by.

"There's one important thing you need to know," Willie said, his voice a whisper. She leaned toward him to hear better. Then Willie's arms clasped onto her waist, and he pulled her tightly against him, gripping her like a vise. Something hard pressed against her side and Elaan realized Willie's gun was jammed in her rib. Her heart hammered and she wanted to run, but she also didn't want him to shoot her. Lijah and Josh seemed to be trying hard not to make sudden moves, Lijah seething silently while Josh balled his fists at his sides.

"Let her go," Lijah said.

"You two are getting off," Willie spat, his hot, foul breath brushing past Elaan's cheek.

"We paid you," Josh said.

"The girl is staying with me," he said. "I'll let her off at St. Louis. You need to get off the train now. Your two-minute window is running out. Use it."

Fear gripped Elaan as Lijah looked out the open

boxcar door. That was supposed to be their freedom. Lijah couldn't leave her with this guy. He couldn't. The pressure in her side eased as Willie aimed the gun at Lijah and Josh. "I said, get off the train."

"Listen," Lijah said, taking a step toward them. "You don't need her. She's just a girl. I can find you someone else. Let her go, and I'll find you a replacement. I'll stay on until I can find you someone else."

Willie cackled. "Boy, there's no one else on this train for you to get."

Lijah hung his head, nodded. "Fine, there's no one else, but please, just let her go. I'll stay here, I'll do whatever you want. Just let her go, please."

Willie scoffed, stabbed the gun at Lijah and said, "Get off the train."

Josh's eyes widened as he looked out the open doorway. "It's the inspector. He's trying to signal you. He wants something. Something's wrong."

Willie strained his neck slightly to catch a glimpse outside. Lijah lurched forward, knocking the gun from Willie's hand and crashing into both Elaan and Willie. She toppled backward onto the old man, her body splayed across his. Elaan scrambled off Willie and turned to see Lijah and Willie tussling on the floor. Lijah punched Willie in the face and she heard something crunch. Blood spurted everywhere. It seemed to be coming from Willie's nose. Lijah hit him in the face again and then grabbed both Willie's hands with one of his and held them.

"Get off me," Willie spat.

Lijah stuck a hand over his mouth and turned to Elaan. "Quick. Get off. Go with Josh."

Elaan stared. She couldn't believe what had just

happened. She saw Willie's gun a few feet away from Lijah. "Get off the train," Lijah said again. "Hurry. Go with Josh."

Josh took a step toward Elaan and grabbed her hand, tugging her off the train. He jumped down first and Elaan was about to go, but she turned back to her brother.

"Hurry up, Lijah," she said.

Her brother shook his head, and Willie tried to shout. Lijah pulled his hand away, punched Willie in the face, and then blocked Willie's mouth again. "Someone has to keep him quiet. Josh knows what to do. Get off the train, now! I'll meet you at our destination."

Josh tugged Elaan's arm, and she fell off the train and into his arms. She was startled, but Josh set her down and started pulling her along. She watched as Lijah hit Willie again, then walked over and picked up the gun. Josh tugged her arm and they started to run. She didn't even see where. A moment later, they were in a little brick building. The mausoleum.

It had an archway, but no door to open or shut. Josh pulled her to the other side of the archway so they were out of sight.

"We just left him," she said to Josh. "How could we leave him?"

Josh bit his lip and said, "I know. I'm sorry. It's just that he told us to get off, and we only had a two-minute window. If we missed it, we'd be stuck on the train. We don't know what checkpoints are coming up next, and we wouldn't be sure how get off, which places were safe."

"But it was OK for Lijah to stay on the train with Willie?"

"I'm sorry," he said. "I know. It's not great that we left Lijah there with Willie, but he told us to go. And he seemed to have it under control. He knows what he's doing."

Elaan blanched. "Lijah had the upper hand for a minute, but we don't know what Willie has up his sleeve."

The freight horn sounded and Elaan looked out. Her heart sank. "The train is leaving, and Lijah's still on there with Willie."

"He told us to get off," Josh said.

"What about Willie?"

"Lijah had gotten the gun away from him," Josh said. Elaan craned her neck to see better, watching the train disappear down the tracks. Elijah was gone. He was going on without them. This was awful. She closed her eyes and began to cry.

7

The train had been gone for at least five minutes, and Elaan had crumpled on the floor for a good cry. She couldn't believe Lijah was still on the train with Willie. What if Willie had gotten the gun back? What if Lijah was dead now? He'd stayed to keep Willie from turning them in. But how was he going to do that? The only way she could think to silence Willie was to kill him. Lijah wasn't a killer. At least she didn't think he was.

Would he become a killer to save her?

Josh rubbed her back as she cried, trying to soothe her. "Elaan," he whispered. "It's going to be dark soon. We need to get out of here and find shelter. People aren't supposed to be out after dark."

Elaan wiped away the tears. The ground was hard, her bottom hurt, and she wasn't sure she had the emotional or physical energy to move. What had her father's note said? Courage wasn't the strength to go on, but going on when you didn't have the strength. Well, she didn't have the strength. But she knew Josh was right. They needed to go. She took a deep breath, nodded at him, and stood. She'd go without strength.

Josh walked over to the archway and peeked out. "I don't see anyone around, so it's probably safe to go." He looked out again. "There's a house in the distance that way. It might be a decent bet."

50

Elaan lifted her backpack, and stared at it. Lijah had said he'd divide their money just in case. Part of her wished he hadn't done it. Maybe he wouldn't have been so quick to tell them to leave if he had needed them with him.

"Spider on your pack?" Josh asked.

She was confused. "What?"

"You're giving your backpack the evil eye, like something's wrong with it. I thought maybe there was a spider or something."

She shook her head, put the pack on, and walked over to join him. "I just wish we hadn't gone without him. I wonder if he hadn't split up the supplies, if maybe he would've just come with us. I mean, Willie's going to talk no matter what. So, what's the point of Lijah riding to the next checkpoint?"

Josh put an arm around Elaan and squeezed her to him. It felt safe and snug. "He must've just thought it was the best move, strategically."

Josh frowned as he gazed outside where the sun was setting in the distance. "We need to go, Elaan."

He slipped his hand into hers and towed her away from the mausoleum. They walked toward the horizon through the cemetery, avoiding tombstones as they trekked in the direction of a lone house surrounded by farmland. They walked quickly, not saying much, both checking to see if anyone was watching them but the area seemed deserted.

They exited the cemetery, crossed a small dirt road, and then walked through a field of dried brown leaves that clearly had been planted in neat rows.

"What is this stuff?" she asked.

"Soybeans, maybe," he said.

She nodded and kept walking. There wasn't much

else to say. She didn't want to talk to Josh. She didn't blame him for Lijah's predicament but she was irritated that he hadn't tried harder to convince Lijah to get off the train. Now, she was here with Josh, and Lijah was stuck with some crazed pedophile. It was hard to believe just yesterday she'd been irritated with Lijah. Just yesterday, she'd actually walked out of a room because Lijah had been in it. She'd give anything to have Lijah here with her. To know he was safe.

A breeze came through, blowing her hair into her face. She brushed it from her eyes and walked quietly beside Josh, the house looming nearer.

"He's going to be OK," Josh said.

"You don't know that," she shot back.

"I don't," Josh said, his voice demurring. "But I'd bet on Lijah any day of the week, and he was clearly in control when we left him."

She didn't respond. She didn't want to argue with him. Being in control when they left was no guarantee Lijah would stay that way. She blew out and focused on the crunch of the plants beneath their sneakers and the little house that was growing larger as they neared it. There was nothing else to say to Josh about Lijah. Elaan eyed the house. It seemed deserted and lonely, the same way she felt. Not that she wasn't glad to have Josh with her, but she was lost without Lijah. He'd promised to take her to their mother, and she knew she'd get there with him. If nothing else, Lijah was one hundred percent rock solid. He was dependable. Having to go it without him frightened her. She and Josh had both viewed Lijah as the leader of their group. Now, he was gone, and she didn't even know if he was safe.

She sighed as they neared the house. The two-story house had a wraparound porch and tall windows. Elaan could see chipped paint on the white wooden slats that made up the house's siding. The windows were closed, but the curtains in many rooms were open. They approached cautiously, not wanting someone to come out and shoot them for trespassing. If the place was empty, it would be the perfect spot to rest for the night. It was sheltered from the weather and seemed enough off the beaten path that they could avoid the military patrols.

They didn't see a car in the carport. Whoever lived here wasn't home at the moment. The question was whether they were coming back or if the place was completely deserted.

Josh took the lead, walking up the stairs to the porch. The wooden boards creaked with each step. Elaan followed, her nerves flaring every time a rickety board groaned beneath their weight. Josh walked along the porch until he reached one of the windows. Elaan joined him, peeking inside.

It was a typical farmhouse room — chairs, a sofa, a little table in the corner, and a cabinet in the back with glass windows that held decorative plates. If she angled her head, Elaan could even see a television directly across from the sofa. The things inside seemed untouched, as if they were set up for museum viewing. She took a step back and examined the layer of dust on the windows. They hadn't been cleaned in a long time. A good sign that the place wasn't in use by anyone.

"Seems empty," she said.

"I'll knock on the door," Josh said. "Just to check. We don't want to try to break in if someone's already in there. You stay here."

He turned to walk the few paces over, but Elaan put her hand on his shoulder. "Wait," she said. "I should go, too."

He raised an eyebrow, and shook his head. "No. We don't know who might answer the door."

He was right about that, but she should still go with him. "I'm a girl," she said, emphasizing the last word. "People are less threatened by girls. If someone answers who's inclined to be hostile, they'll be less hostile with me than with you, right?"

"I can deal with hostility, Elaan," he said. "Plus, we're both young. People understand young people who are lost, especially in times like these."

Elaan bit her lip. She didn't want him to go to the door. She looked back in the window. The furniture inside was probably dusty too, though it was hard to tell through the grimy view. She couldn't imagine anyone being in there. Knocking was really just a precaution, but she was a little worried what would happen if someone did answer. "What if the person who answers the door is sick?" she asked. She didn't want Josh to be turned into a carrier.

He smiled at her, sighed. "It's a good point, and one I've thought of. But if I were alone, I'd knock on the door, and deal with the consequences. I'm not going to let you take that risk when I'm here with you. Besides, what if the person who answers the door is like —" he paused, as if deciding whether to continue. "What if it's someone like Willie?"

The sound of that name made her cringe. She'd spent one night on a train with him, and thoughts of his creepiness would forever haunt her. She nodded, so Josh spoke again. "I don't want someone to grab you, pull you inside, and lock the door."

Whoa! That wasn't what she'd expected to hear, but it made sense. Still, she was torn. It was brave of him to take the risk to protect her, but she didn't want him to be turned into a carrier, or worse, injured by a psycho inhabitant, just because he was trying to help her. That was too much of a price to pay.

"Why don't we knock together?" she said, grabbing his hand.

"OK," he said, rolling his eyes. "Ms. Stubborn, we'll go together."

Holding hands, they walked over to the wooden door, and Josh used his free hand to knock. "Anyone home," he called out.

They waited and heard nothing. Elaan saw no one in the immediate area. She didn't want to be spied by a neighbor who might call the police. Though, there weren't any neighbors, as far she could see. Just farmland. Rotting fields and nothingness.

"Anyone here?" Josh called out, rapping on the door again. They waited and still no response.

"Try the door," Elaan said.

Josh released her hand and tried the doorknob. It didn't budge. "Locked," he said. "Stay here. I'll go around back and see if there's an open door. If it's not open, maybe I can jimmy it."

He started to walk away and Elaan followed. "Josh, I don't think we should split up."

He stopped and faced her. He wore a glower, but his eyes were sympathetic. After a moment of consideration, he sighed and turned to start walking again. "Alright. Come on."

They took the porch all the way around to the back of the house, where they found a sliding glass door leading to the kitchen. A battered screen door stood just outside the glass one. There was a small hole in the lower left side, where a squirrel or mouse or something had gnawed through, but then realized it was pointless, as it couldn't penetrate the glass door.

Josh tugged on the sliding screen door. It didn't move. It was locked. He knelt down, reached into the hole, and began ripping the screen.

"What are you doing?" Elaan asked.

"Just going to pull this out, and see if the inner door is open." He tugged at the screen until he'd ripped it the height of the door, and the screen hung from its frame like a curtain. He tugged on the glass door. It opened.

Josh smiled, pulling the door all the way back. "After you, milady," he said.

8

Willie was sitting in the corner of the boxcar, his eyes slits and his jaw a solid ridge of anger. Lijah watched him carefully, the gun trained on his torso. Lijah stood about ten feet away from Willie, so he would see a move when Willie made one. And Lijah was sure Willie planned to make a move. It was a question of when, not if.

Lijah had the gun and the upper hand for the moment, but that would all change the instant they hit another checkpoint. Lijah had given it careful thought. He knew the longest they'd gone without a checkpoint was four hours. That was the most time he could expect to have, but he didn't know if one was coming sooner than that. It had been about fifty minutes since Josh and Elaan had gotten off the train. Lijah's plan was to wait another twenty minutes, and then make Willie jump from the train.

That meant Willie would have a half an hour to find shelter before curfew. It also meant Willie wouldn't be able to contact anyone about what or whom he'd seen until morning. If his plan worked, Lijah could ride the train another hour, then get off before the next checkpoint. Then, he'd be like Josh and Elaan, going it on foot, or via stolen car, the rest of the trip.

However, getting off an hour after Willie also

meant Lijah would definitely be violating the curfew. If spotted, he'd definitely get arrested or shot. Though, he didn't know whether the curfew was enforced. Willie had mentioned it, but was he referring only to the big cities? What if in Middle America, they just didn't have the resources to patrol the countryside? That meant his plan for Willie would go astray, too. Willie might walk up to the next cop he saw and tell him he'd seen fugitives escaping on a train heading to St. Louis. He might even tell the cop where Elaan and Josh had gotten off.

He sighed. The best thing for them all would be if Willie were dead. But Lijah couldn't kill another human being just because it was what was best for himself. He didn't want to be like that, like the people he was running from. People who had decided it would be better for the world if Lijah and those like him were dead. Lijah couldn't kill Willie just because it would make his life easier.

Now, if Willie attacked him, and it were Lijah or Willie, Lijah was certain he'd choose his own life. But without those circumstances, making Willie jump from the train seemed the best bet. If Willie did it right, he'd be OK. Lijah wouldn't have killed him. Though, if Willie did it wrong…. That was the part that worried Lijah. If Willie did it wrong, and he got under the wheels somehow or landed wrong, he'd die. It would still be as if Lijah had killed him. Forcing Willie out could be a death sentence as much as shooting him.

Lijah shook his head. No, Willie was wily enough to get safely to the ground. The man had survived this long. Surely, he could survive a jump and a night in the elements. And Lijah could do fine in the wilderness. The key thing was not getting caught.

"Thinking 'bout how you gonna kill me?" Willie asked, his voice hard.

Lijah stared and shook his head. "I don't want to kill you, Willie," he admitted. "All I want. All I've wanted this whole trip is to be done with you so I can go on my merry way. But you've made it so we're stuck with each other a bit longer."

"You can get off this train, and I won't tell nobody 'bout you," Willie said, a hopeful gleam in his eye.

"Willie, if you'd done one thing you ever said you would, I'd make that deal with you and hop off right now. But all you've ever done is double-cross me."

Willie shook his head. "That was the lust that did it to me, boy," he said. "I wasn't in my right mind with such a pretty, nubile young thing on board. But now that she's gone, I can think clearly. I did you wrong, and you have every right not to trust me, but I promise you, I'm on the straight and narrow now. You can leave me be, and I'll forget this all happened."

Willie stood there, pretending to be earnest and sad. Lijah had half a mind to believe him. Lust was a powerful thing, even when you knew you were in the wrong. He'd wanted Josh and hurt his sister because of it. But even if he believed Willie meant what he said, Lijah couldn't afford to trust him. Willie was old enough to know better, and Lijah was sure it hadn't been lust driving his decisions; it had been the belief that he could get away with taking Elaan without repercussions.

That had been a foolish belief, because it had thrown everyone's plans into disarray. Now, all four of them were stuck doing things they wished they didn't have to do.

"Willie," Lijah said. "I can let bygones be bygones. You and I will be all copasetic. You just have to get off of this train."

9

Willie bared his teeth and squinted. "You're tryin'ta kick me offa my train," he growled. "It don't work that way, boy."

Lijah held the gun out farther, stiffened his arm, a hardness in his eyes. "I'm afraid it's going to work that way tonight." Lijah glanced at the boxcar door to his left and then back at Willie. There was no use in waiting. He needed to do this now, because Willie wasn't going to go easy. "I'm going to open that door, and you're going to jump."

"While the train is moving?" Willie asked.

Lijah nodded.

"That'll kill me just as good as my gun that you're pointing at me."

"It's my gun, now, Willie," Lijah said, his voice resolute, stronger than he'd expected. "And the jump won't kill you. Just pay attention and try to go into a roll away from the train."

"And if instead of going away from the train, I get crushed by its wheels? You'd really kill me, boy?" Willie asked.

Lijah kept the gun held steady, despite his irritation at Willie for calling him 'boy.' He wasn't sure if Willie was trying to rile him on purpose, so he'd lose his concentration, or if he was just so mad at the situation he didn't care about insulting the man holding a gun on him. Lijah took a deep breath and spoke calmly. "Willie, you have to get off this train. If you die, then it's on your head. You set this in motion when you backed out of our deal and tried to take my sister."

Willie stood there, seething, his breath heavy, his beady eyes trained on Lijah. They both trembled from the motion of the train, but both were firm in all the ways that counted: their stances, eye contact and resolve etched into their faces.

Lijah lifted the gun slightly higher. He needed to check his watch, which was on the hand holding the gun. His eyes darted to the ticking hands, and he realized it had been an hour. Keeping the gun trained on Willie the entire time, he edged to the door. Willie grinned at him. It took a moment for Lijah to realize what had Willie so jazzed. Lijah would need both hands to open the door.

"Go ahead," Willie said. "Open the door to throw me off the train."

Lijah gritted his teeth, but said nothing. He needed a minute to think. He had to get Willie off the train, and the only way to do that was to open the door, but if he set the gun down Willie would pounce on him. He'd bested Willie earlier today. But did he want to bet his own life that he could best him again? On a moving train? Even if he managed to get the door open, what if Willie just barreled into him? The force would knock Lijah right off the train. If the older man ran straight at him, Willie wouldn't be able to stop and would end up off the train with Lijah. But if he ran at the right angle, he could maintain his momentum, knock Lijah out the door, and remain safe inside. The guy had taught science, so he was probably pretty decent at math, too, and could figure out the angle he'd need so that he stayed on the train while Lijah went barreling over the side.

Lijah wanted to close his eyes and think, to block out the world for a minute so he could get a clearer picture of what to do. But he couldn't do that. Willie was over there considering how to get the gun away from him.

Then it hit Lijah what to do. He took several steps backward, away from the door handle. "Come over to the door."

Willie hesitated, and Lijah, who'd been holding the gun near his body, aimed it square at Willie's his chest. "I said, come over to the door."

Willie pursed his lips and glared, but complied. The older man walked until he was parallel with the door, but only a few feet in front of Lijah.

"Stop," Lijah said firmly, though his heart hammered inside his chest.

Willie stopped.

"You're gonna open the door," Lijah said.

Willie shook his head. "No, I'm not."

Lijah snorted. "Now is not the time to get defiant," he said, brandishing the gun.

Willie shook his head again. "If I were to attack you, maybe you shoot me and tell yourself it's self-defense. Maybe you can live with that. Maybe you won't have nightmares every day for the rest of your life about killing me. I think you would. I think shooting me, even if you gave yourself the lame excuse that you did it as self-defense, would haunt you. It would make you know what a truly awful human being you were for taking the life of another man. Another of God's creatures."

Lijah swallowed but said nothing. Willie had the

trace of a smirk on his lips.

"But I know you wouldn't shoot me in cold blood. You wouldn't simply murder me. It's not who you are. If it were, you would've shot me and got off the train with your sister. You didn't. Even this plan to dump me on the side of the tracks is designed to let me live. So, I'm not opening this door."

Willie stood there, smug. No smile at the moment, but his beard couldn't shroud the clear satisfaction that rushed through him with his pronouncement.

Lijah was frustrated, because Willie was right. If it came down to Willie or Lijah, a life or death battle, Lijah would easily pick himself. But to simply murder someone in cold blood. That wasn't him. Still, he needed Willie off the train.

"Willie," Lijah said, shaking his head, and then smiling. "You're good at reading people and you've assessed a lot about me. You're right. I'm not a cold-blooded murderer. But you've miscalculated just a bit. I wouldn't do something to kill you just because you're here. But I am ruthless in certain ways. I want you off of this train, and I'm going to make it happen. So, you can open this door, like I asked, and jump off the train in one piece, or I can shoot you in the foot, both feet if necessary, and let you deal with that pain, while I open the door, and then throw you off this train, quite lame. It's up to you."

The satisfaction drained away and Willie narrowed his eyes. "You could hit an artery in my foot. I could bleed to death."

"Then I suggest you hold still when I shoot," Lijah said. "Because you're right about one thing. If you come at me, I will shoot for the heart and you will die. If you make it a choice between you or me, I'm choosing me. So open the goddamn door and get off this train, or I'm going to shoot you in the foot and then throw you off."

The two men stood there another minute sizing each other up, when finally, Willie lifted his hands, grabbed the door's handle, and slid the door back. The sudden whoosh of air startled Lijah and he blinked.

It was just long enough for Willie to take advantage, bending low like a linebacker and hurling himself at Lijah. Not enough time to react, Lijah fell hard on the train floor, the wind knocked out of him. Somehow, he kept his hand clamped tightly around the gun. Willie grabbed hold of the gun and tried to pull it free, but Lijah held on. Willie was on top of him, so Lijah bucked his abdomen to dislodge the old man. The move failed, and only served to further enrage Willie.

Lijah knew he couldn't hold on to the weapon much longer if Willie continued like this. Lijah jerked his upper body forward, slamming his head directly into Willie's. It was brain-splittingly painful. Whoever had told him that it hurts the person who isn't expecting the head-butt more than the person who's giving it was wrong. Stars floated in Lijah's vision. He could barely see, straining to keep his eyes open.

Willie wasn't grabbing for the gun anymore. One hand held his head, and the man had tipped backward onto the railcar's floor. Taking this small opportunity, Lijah punched Willie, knocking him farther away. Lijah scooted across the train floor, keeping the gun in his hand, and trying to focus his blurry vision on his adversary. Willie wasn't done, and retreating was probably a bad move. Men like Willie understood only one thing: unbridled aggression and attempts for domination. But Lijah could barely see, and he wasn't going to head for Willie like this, even if he was the one with the gun.

Lijah was seeing double now and regretting his head-butting idea. Willie lunged toward him, and Lijah knew exactly what Willie wanted: the gun. As long as he had it, Willie would come for it, and that meant Lijah would have to shoot him and kill him. Only, he wasn't sure he was ready to do that. His life was dependent on him keeping this gun away from Willie, but he still wasn't sure he could shoot his foe. That was when the idea popped into his head.

Willie was on Lijah, grabbing at his arms, trying to dislodge the gun. So Lijah turned, eyeing the open cargo door, and tossed the gun toward it. He prayed it hadn't gone too far, and that Willie would take the bait. As if the silent prayer had gone from his mind directly to God's ear, Willie let go of him and ran for the gun. Lijah ran, too, at an angle. As Willie picked up the gun, Lijah slammed into him, knocking the older man through the open cargo door. Lijah heard an angry scream as Willie went flying off the train. Unable to stop his forward momentum, Lijah crashed into the side wall of the rail car.

His entire body reverberated off the metal wall and he fell backward, with a thud. He was alive. He was banged up, but alive.

Lijah lay there on the cold metal floor for a few minutes, the adrenaline leaving him, his body cooling down from the fight-or-flight response. The adrenaline gone, the pain from his battle with Willie flared. His entire body throbbed and his head ached. But he was alone, done with Willie. He stood, finally, walking over to the door, grabbing the handle with both hands, and pulling it shut. Then, he lay down. He had to rest. He wasn't sure how long before the next checkpoint, but he needed a few minutes to regroup, and then he had to come up with a plan.

10

Staring out the living room window, Elaan saw nothing but empty fields and the setting sun.

"Do you think people still live here?" she asked.

He shrugged. "It seems pretty deserted," he said, looking at the dust-covered furniture. "That's why we tried it."

She nodded. She wasn't sure why she asked him. Her mind was still racing, still replaying the events of today. Still trying to make sense of everything. Lijah gone. She had no idea if he was safe or if a military patrol had caught him. And if they had, they would surely kill him. He'd given her the map back, which was good, because then they wouldn't know where he was going. But had he traced it like she suggested. If so, authorities might figure out where Lijah was headed.

Elaan followed Josh through the deserted old farmhouse. They'd entered through the kitchen in the back but hadn't spent long there. Josh thought it important to search the house and make sure it was completely empty. He stationed her at the living room window to keep watch in case anyone approached. Elaan didn't think Josh would find anyone upstairs. The hardwood floors were also covered in a thick layer of dust, except tiny footprints, which she suspected were from rats. Though, she hadn't seen any vermin in the few minutes they'd been in the house.

The place smelled stale and mildewy. She shuddered at the thought that in this new reality, stale and mildewy was a good thing. It meant the place actually was deserted. Little knickknacks set about the room — cat figurines, doilies, crocheted throws — made it seem like an old person's house.

Josh came downstairs, declaring the upstairs clear. "We should go to the kitchen and see what food they have so we can eat, and figure out what to take with us tomorrow."

Elaan acknowledged she'd heard him but didn't speak. She followed Josh back to the kitchen. It had a dirty linoleum floor and yellow walls with a country border at the top. The cabinets were white with little gold knobs. It seemed quaint. The refrigerator was silent, lacking the hum of electricity running through it. Probably no power here. She went over to a light switch and flicked it on. Nothing.

"Guess they didn't pay the bill," Josh joked.

She smiled. "Didn't pay because they were dead, or had the power stopped working because the people who ran the power plant were dead?" Elaan shivered. She wasn't sure she wanted to know.

Josh sighed as he took in the room. "We should get stuff before it gets dark. I don't want to use the flashlights and draw attention to the fact that someone's roaming the house."

Elaan nodded. Without another word, they went to cabinets and opened them up. There were lots of cans: beans, chili, pineapple chunks, mandarin oranges, and a bevy of soups. Ideal for dinner but not for taking with them. The cans would load down their packs, and they'd need a can opener. She scanned the room to see if there was one lying on a counter, when she heard Josh yelp behind her. She turned in time to see something gray and fuzzy scurry across the floor and into the other room.

"You OK?" Elaan asked.

Josh's face was red. "Yeah, I'm just startled." He tried to feign that he wasn't bothered by seeing whatever had darted out of the cupboard. "I guess the cereal and boxed food in here was eaten by that rat and its family."

Rats. She wondered how many of them there were. "Is it safe to sleep here, if there are rats?" Hadn't she seen a movie where a bunch of rats attacked a man and gnawed on his flesh?

Josh shrugged. "They're probably just in the kitchen, where there's food, not the bedrooms."

That made sense. Josh walked over to the sink and tried to turn it on, but nothing happened. "Water's off, too," he said. "But I think I'd rather be in than out. It's almost October, and I'm pretty sure regional lows for this area are in the forties. It seems like it's already unseasonably cold." He glanced out the window over the sink. "I certainly don't want to be out there with whatever is crawling through the fields."

Inside was better, but the idea of rats biting or crawling over her inside was a bit creepy, too. Her eyes wandered to the spot where the furry creature had darted past.

Josh gave her a sympathetic look, and said, "I didn't see anything unusual when I went through the first time, but let's check out the house again, together. I mean, rats are one thing, but we need to evaluate what we want to do if there's a family of raccoons nesting here. They're pretty vicious."

She tried not to cringe, as she was pretty sure he'd been trying to make her feel better by offering to check out the house. But raccoons. God only knew what could be living in this house. She nodded, and followed him out of the kitchen and up the stairs to hallway with four doors coming off of it.

The first door opened to a bedroom with an unmade queen-size bed. There was a dresser, TV, and typical accoutrements. The room seemed like that of an adult's. There was nothing frilly or childlike such as teddy bears or posters. The dresser had some pill bottles on it. Elaan stood in the doorway, while Josh went in and opened the closet door, seeking any signs of infestation. He got on the floor and peeked beneath the bed. "Nothing here," he said.

They did the same on the rest of the floor. There was one child's bedroom and another room that appeared to be for guests. It had a full-size bed, fully made, and a desk with a lamp, but no dresser or anything that a person who lived in the room would have. The closet in the room had pillows, sheets, and extra blankets. The fourth door had been to a bathroom. However, Josh reminded Elaan, that without water, they wouldn't be able to flush.

They found no signs of animals outside of the kitchen. Elaan breathed easier as she and Josh went back to the kitchen. They noticed a small pantry closet and opened it. Jackpot. Sitting on top of a large plastic container were two 24 packs of bottled water. Once they moved the water and opened the container, they found food. Elaan suspected the animals hadn't been able to get inside the box because of the water's weight.

They found Ritz crackers, granola bars, an inordinate amount of boxed raisins, individually wrapped PB&J sandwich bars, and mini bags of trail mix.

"We can't take all this water with us, so let's go ahead and take a bottle each to wash up with, and then let's eat."

Elaan agreed easily, and soon they'd found a can opener and utensils. They ate at the dining room table, directly from the cans. The food had been cold, but Elaan had been hungry enough that she didn't care. After they finished eating, they took their food trash outside to avoid attracting vermin.

Josh suggested they go upstairs and get ready before it got completely dark. "Boxcar Willie double-crossed us," Josh said. The mention of Willie's name caused her to blanch.

"I know that better than anyone," she said, still bitter about Lijah.

He put a hand on her shoulder. "I'm sorry," he said. "I should have started differently. I know what happened with Lijah is still fresh. What I meant was, even though Willie lied to us about some things, I'm not sure he lied about the curfew. We'd heard Martial Law had been implemented, and even though we haven't seen anyone and even though this seems like the middle of nowhere, we can't assume curfew isn't being enforced. We should try to keep as low a profile as possible. If someone sees light in this abandoned house, they might come check it out."

Elaan wrinkled her nose and folded her arms. "I know what you're saying, but do you really think the patrols randomly search the country? It seems like they'd stay in the cities. I mean, they have to be short of men with so many people dead from the virus."

Josh bristled at the mention of the word virus. Or was that her imagination. She was safe from it, but exposure to it meant something entirely different for him.

He swallowed and said, "I don't want to take the chance. Especially since we're not far from the train station. Though, we're definitely on the Indiana side. If Willie told them we're going to St. Louis, they're probably searching for us down that way. I think it's best to just lie low here and be extra cautious."

Elaan rubbed her chin, not entirely convinced. She didn't like the idea of being in complete darkness in a strange house. She'd like to light a candle or use the flashlights or something, but nodded to Josh that it was fine.

"Hey," Josh said. "I know it hasn't gone the way we wanted it to, but we're going to be OK."

She frowned. What about Lijah? Would he be OK? Elaan closed her eyes and thought, *God, please let him be OK.*

"Lijah's going to be OK, too," Josh said, as if he could read her mind. "Come on. Let's get upstairs. I think you'll feel better if you get some rest. I didn't sleep that well on the train. I can't imagine you did, either."

11

Josh and Elaan had headed upstairs to get ready for bed for the night. They were in what appeared to be the guest bedroom. The walls were painted a pale lavender and Elaan was sure it would be pretty in the morning, when the light streamed in. At present, it was pretty dark. There were no curtains, and the light from the moon had offered enough of a glow that they didn't to crash into things as they got ready for bed.

Given that they'd been forced to separate from Lijah, they decided it best they stay together. Josh had been a gentleman and offered to sleep on the floor, but Elaan said it made more sense for them to both get a good night's sleep and share the bed.

To preserve the cleanliness of their clothes, Elaan was wearing her underpants and a long shirt she'd pulled from her bag. She'd used a little bit of the bottled water to wipe down the armpits of the shirt, trying to extend its freshness a couple of days. Josh had done the same.

It was a little awkward climbing into bed with Josh, half dressed, but she had not been able to think of a better solution.

Elaan and Josh lay next to each other in the bed, but not touching. Two fleece blankets covered them, leaving Elaan warm and toasty. This was better than the train, where she'd been bone cold no matter what she did. Though, perhaps it had been partly psychological; Willie's leers had chilled her as much as the temperature.

Elaan closed her eyes and tried to clear her mind so she could get some sleep. But it was too early. It was probably a little after seven o'clock. Even with her poor sleep on the train, her mind still raced.

A hand grazed the outside of her thigh.

"Oh, I'm sorry," Josh said, and his hand slid away. "I just was going to hold your hand. I swear. I didn't mean to, um, violate your space."

She laughed and reached toward him, finding his hand. "It's OK," she said. "Honest mistake." She gave his hand a squeeze. Part of her thought it nice he was being a gentleman, but another part of her wondered why he found it so easy to be gentlemanly.

"Listen, we'll get up in the morning and start walking west," Josh said. "We'll get there eventually."

Elaan sucked in a breath, not sure she believed. "And Lijah? What if they got him, Josh?"

The bed trembled as he shook his head. "I don't think they did. Lijah's strong and resourceful."

"So resourceful that he can evade the military?"

"Don't count him out," Josh said. "You didn't see him in quarantine. I was less than stellar when I found out about the vaccine. It's disturbing when you learn the life you know, the one you thought you knew, is over. That your savior is really a curse. It messes with your mind, and your thoughts go dark. But not Lijah. Never once did he give in to bleak thinking. Never once did he let me. That kind of resolve shows strength, fortitude, and endurance. Lijah will figure it out. He'll be fine."

Elaan turned to see his silhouette in the darkness. Even in the glow of the rising moon, Josh was handsome. "What was it like for the two of you?" she asked. "Being quarantined together?"

Josh didn't answer for a moment. She heard the sound of their breathing mingled with the song of crickets that drifted in from outside. Finally he spoke, his voice quiet. "It made us lifelong friends. Being in there was normal at first. It was simple and normal." He paused and chuckled. "I keep saying normal, but it's sort of the only word that comes to mind. It seemed normal back then. Because even though the world had changed, we thought we were on the cusp of, essentially, a cure. No, it couldn't save those who had Helnoan, but it would stop its spread. Things would go back to normal, and then, in a second, it all changed. Nothing would go back to normal. We wouldn't get sick, but if we came into contact with the sick, we'd make others sick. And then we'd be sterile. For me, it all shifted so quickly. Way too quickly. From hope to despair."

He breathed out, and shivered, as if the memory of it all was too haunting to relive. "After they realized the vaccine was bad, my dad took every precaution to make sure no one found out we'd been given the vaccine. It had been tested on a handful of soldiers, and my dad said the government took them all to Facility One. So, our dads' big concern at first was that no one would find out and kill us. My dad kept saying he'd fix it, but not to worry about the fix because we could be safe if we just got into scientist housing. Getting into the housing would give us time. Only, if the government found out, we'd be dead.

And that's when Lijah and I bonded. We both knew it was possible that the government would find out, that we would be erased from the world without a second thought. So, we talked to each other. Nonstop. We told each other everything. It was almost as if both of us realized we might be dead and we wanted another person, at least one other person, to know who we were. Not superficially, not a little bit, but to truly know and understand us to our core."

He swallowed, and his eyes searched her face for assurance. "If there's one other person who knows you, it means your life wasn't a waste, right?"

Elaan squeezed his hand, finally understanding the bond Josh and Lijah shared, and why he seemed so hesitant to break it. Why he was so willing to yield to Lijah's demands that he stay away from her. Not just because it was dangerous, but also because Lijah mattered. Lijah was the only other person who really understood him. Not just what it was like to be in his shoes, but him. She gave Josh a reassuring smile. She understood exactly what he meant.

"Anyway," he said. "That's what it was like in the quarantine. It would have been a lonely experience alone. But Lijah and I had each other. And I'm telling you not to worry about him. When things seem dark, that's when he turns on the light. He had the Willie situation figured out, and I'm sure he'll be fine and get to your mom's. In fact, I'll bet you five bucks that he's already at your mom's place when we get there."

Elaan laughed. "Can we bet toilet paper instead?"

"Alright, one roll," he joked back.

Elaan shook her head. These last two days were the kind you either laughed or cried about. Josh had made her laugh, but part of her really just wanted a good cry. She stared up at the ceiling. It would be completely dark soon, and she wasn't ready for that. She wasn't ready to be claimed by darkness.

"You should try to sleep," he said.

"Can't," she admitted. "My mind is too busy." She took a deep breath, and said, "Talk to me for a bit. Tell me stories. Talk to me the way you did Lijah when you were quarantined. The way you talked to each other when you didn't want to feel alone."

Josh released her hand for a second, and the mattress shook slightly. He rolled on his side to face her, leaned forward and pressed his lips to hers. Heat flooded her cheeks, and his warm skin pressed close to her. For a moment, she was lost in the feel of him, then he pulled away. "I talked to Lijah, man to man, in a way that builds a bond of friendship that's unbreakable," he said. "I want to talk to you in a way that builds a different kind of bond." He lifted his hand and stroked her cheek. "I'll talk to you about anything you want, but we're not just friends, OK?"

She nodded, his fingers still grazing her cheek, leaving warm streaks.

"Why don't I start with the stuff you asked me about the other night?" Josh said, removing his hand from her face and rolling onto his back.

Elaan raised an eyebrow, though she was sure he couldn't see it. "What stuff?"

"Where my dad gets all his gadgets. You asked me if he was a spy or something."

"Is he?"

Josh laughed, then found her hand again, pulling it into his own. "No," he said. "But mild-mannered, cookie-baking, PTA President Jennifer Wells was."

Elaan's mouth popped open as the shock of his

words set in. "Are you serious?"

"Umm, yes," he said. "She told people she worked as a translator for the State Department. A lot of spies say they work for the State Department, and while technically true, it's part of their cover."

"She went on missions and stuff?"

He laughed again. "No, that would have made her job more exciting and probably left her less time to volunteer at my school. Nope, she had various jobs in the agency. At the end, she was in charge of some covert ops program that I don't know a lot about. Before that, she was in the tech department. She was the real-world equivalent to Q, who was James Bond's tech guy. She designed gadgets for spies to use. You're not supposed to take certain documents and tools home, but she had a high enough clearance to bring home some stuff most people wouldn't have access to. She was also considered essential personnel. She had an emergency kit that had everything she would need if she had to leave and go to a safe house. My dad took the kit after she got sick. That's probably where he got most of the stuff. I'm sure there's protocol to retrieve those kits, but with the virus and everything else that was going on, it must have slipped through the cracks."

Elaan was stunned. It was hard to believe she knew someone whose mother was a high-level CIA operative. And he knew about it. He hadn't talked about his mother much back at the SPU. She'd assumed it was too depressing, just like it had been for her. Missing someone so much sometimes made it hard to dredge it all up for others. But had his reticence been because of her job? His mother was a spy, someone who lied for a living. Elaan had trouble wrapping her mind around the idea. Yes, spies existed in real life and not just the movies; spies just weren't people she knew.

"Did you always know she was a spy?"

Josh shrugged, his hand pulling slightly on hers with the move. "I didn't know when I was younger, but my mother told me, before I left for college."

"Were you shocked?"

"Not entirely," he said. "I'd seen the stuff she brought home. I'd been to her office a few times. Everything I saw seemed more interesting and mysterious than what a translator should have had access to."

He'd seen things. She wondered what kind of things, but then remembered his special talent. "You saw stuff and your photographic memory detected later it wasn't kosher."

He sighed and said, "I actually have to view it a certain way for the photographic memory to kick in, but I knew enough to know that what she did was more complicated than what she said."

Elaan nodded. She paused, and then decided to say what was on her mind, the thing that had been bothering her ever since Lijah had told her about it. "You never told me that you have a photographic memory."

He took a moment before he spoke, his brows crunching together slightly. "I generally don't tell people," he said, finally. "Sometimes, people put up walls after you tell them something like that."

She stared. That didn't make sense.

It was as if he could read her thoughts. "It's not people's first reaction," he admitted. "At first they think it's cool, and they go through this testing phase where they're like, 'Hey, do you remember this? What was on the paper I just showed you?' But that wears off eventually. Then, they move into suspicion and distrust. They're reluctant to show you stuff because they think it's there with you, forever. I don't like being in that place with people. So, it's better just not to tell anyone."

Except Lijah, she thought, but kept the words inside.

"I'm glad you know. I wasn't actively trying to hide it. I just didn't want you to shut me out or think I was weird or something."

Elaan laughed. "You told me about your Teenage Mutant Ninja Turtle collection, but thought I'd find photographic memory weird?"

"Lijah said you liked TMNT, that you were always watching it."

She laughed even harder now. "Because I was babysitting the twin boys next door, Fred and Frank. They loved that movie."

"So, were you just teasing when you told me Raph was your favorite?"

"No, I do like Raphael best," she admitted. "There are just other movies I think I'd rather watch."

"Like *The Princess Bride*?"

"Yes. Or *Ever After*," she said. "Something where things end well and people live happily ever after. Something different from how the world is now. The world right now is filled with a disease that kills people by the millions, most of them good people who've done nothing wrong. The world right now is a government that hunts you down to experiment on you or kill you, depending on your genetic makeup."

Josh put an arm around her. "I know it's been

hard these past few days, but you're gonna be OK, Elaan," he said in a reassuring tone. "We're going to be OK."

She took a deep breath and sank into his arms, relishing the safety of his embrace. She wanted to feel safe again, like the world wasn't falling apart. She leaned into him, and inhaled. He smelled slightly earthy and sweaty, and for some reason, she liked that. She blew out, her breath landing on his chest, and he tremored afterward.

"We should get some sleep," he said, pulling away from her. She heard him swallow and then take in a couple of long, steady breaths.

She didn't like that he'd pulled away. He said he wanted to be more than friends, but he was letting her go when she needed to be held. She snuggled close to him, resting her head on his shoulder. "I can sleep like this," she said, placing a hand on his chest, enjoying the thump of his heartbeat under her palm.

He wrapped an arm around her. "Sure," he said. "So long as you're comfortable."

"I am," she said quickly, enjoying the warmth of his body next to hers. "Thanks for being here with me. I know you could've gone on your own, but it means a lot that you stayed with us, and that you're coming with me to Illinois."

He put his hand on top of hers, and his chest rose as he inhaled. "I'm glad I came, too."

12

In the morning, Elaan woke to sunshine streaming in. The watch she'd placed on the nightstand read six-thirty. She felt refreshed, especially since she'd slept so poorly on the train.

The space beside her was empty. Josh was gone. She sat up, telling herself not to panic. He probably just went to the bathroom. Across the room, where they'd set their clothes to dry, she saw his pants were gone. His shirt, however was still draped over a chair.

Elaan heard noise coming from the next room and called, "Josh?"

"Yeah," he called back. "One second."

She climbed out of the bed, put on her pants, and searched her bag for something other than the camouflage shirt. She heard the door creak open as she rummaged in the bag. She looked up to see Josh standing in the doorway wearing clothes she'd never seen before. "Where'd you get those?"

"Last bedroom. They were in the drawers. They seemed clean, so I figured it would be a good idea to swap these out for the fatigues." He held up an empty duffle bag. "This was in one of the other rooms. I figured we could use another bag."

"Won't it be heavy? Slow us down?"

Josh sighed, walked over to the bed, and sat down. "Well, yeah it will be heavier, but I think it's worth it."

He closed his eyes for a second, then opened them. "From the map and my best-guess, it's about two hundred thirty miles from here to Dahinda. If the average person walks one mile in twenty minutes, that's forty-six hundred minutes, or roughly seventy-seven hours. Even walking ten hours a day, that puts us there in eight days, and probably exhausted and near starvation. And ten hours a day is being generous. I'd say eight hours of walking to be on the safe side, putting us closer to a ten-day trip. How likely is it that we'll find decent shelter for that many days in a row?"

Elaan stared, not clear where he was going with this. "What are you saying?"

"I think we should try to steal a car. With a car, it's a four-hour trip, not a week and a half."

Elaan raised both brows. "How are we supposed to steal a car? You guys nixed the idea earlier. Lijah said most cars need a chip to start."

He nodded, and crossed the room to her. "I know," he said, touching her shoulder. "But being out here isn't like being in a city. A lot of people are dead, and their heirs are dead, and their things just are. They're like this house — unoccupied and forgotten about. It's possible there's a car in a garage somewhere that has a full tank of gas, a set of keys, and no occupants. Any car with decent mileage and full tank means we won't even have to stop for gas."

Elaan lifted her hand to her chin and sat on the edge of the desk. "So, where do you think we'll find an abandoned car before it gets dark?"

"I checked out some of the other rooms while you were sleeping and found some binoculars and a fifty-state atlas. The map is a little more detailed, and I think if we walk along the highway, we might spot a house or two that's abandoned. However, the ones closest to the roads are also the likeliest ones to have been looted already. This one here is a little off the beaten path. But I still think it's worth a shot. I mean, a few hours versus ten days is a huge difference. Plus, we're going to really have to figure out food if we can't find a car. We don't have a way to carry ten days of food with us."

Elaan nodded. He was right. "But you still want to take the extra duffel?"

Josh shrugged. "It would allow us to carry more rations, but it's going to be heavier. So, it's a tradeoff." He paused. "Do you know any, like, wilderness survival tips? You know, stuff about edible plants and herbs."

Elaan burst into a full belly laugh. "Um, no. You should've gotten stranded with Lijah. He could've helped you. I have zero outdoor skills. If you rely on me, we'll probably eat the first poisonous bush we come across."

He chuckled. "OK, Elaan doesn't have a secret life as a survivalist," he said. "Well, neither do I. So, we'll wing it. Why don't you look around, see if there are any extra clothes you want to take with you? Try to find stuff that's warm and would dry quickly if it got wet. Fleece, polyester, synthetic fabrics. We don't know what kind of weather we'll get."

Ugh. The weather. She hadn't thought about that.

"Hey, don't worry," Josh said. "We can do this. We just need to prepare." Elaan managed a smile and Josh went on. "Just see if there's anything that's a good fit for you, finish getting ready, and then come down. I'll start packing some light food and water.

The map showed a couple of ponds and creeks on the way, so we can try to refill there if we have to walk the whole way. I'll poke around outside. I think I saw a shed. Maybe there's something we can use to make the trip easier."

Elaan sighed. Walking for a week or stealing a car. Neither seemed her idea of fun. But truth be told, nothing in this post-virus world had been much fun, so odds were low things would suddenly turn fun now.

13

Elaan had searched for things they could use on their journey, but found herself reluctant to take anything. It still felt like stealing, even though the home's owners were likely dead. The notion of taking other people's clothes also gave her pause, but for the ick factor mostly. She didn't want to wear something that had touched someone else's skin, especially if she wasn't clear on who they were or how clean their things were. She finally convinced herself to take two fleece zip pullovers. The weather was turning colder, and she'd want something warm if they didn't find a decent place to stay overnight. The fleece was light, but a bit bulkier than some of the other stuff in her bag. So, it would be perfect for the extra duffle.

Staring at the pullovers, Elaan still had misgivings about taking them. Perhaps after ten days of wandering, she'd be less picky, but now, having been decently fed, she wasn't in the best of spirits about pilfering clothing.

She was sitting on the bed cornrowing one of the last sections of her hair. While she generally liked to wear her hair out, the realities of walking for ten days made her opt for a more practical hairstyle.

She heard footsteps on the stairs and realized Josh must be back. He'd found a wagon outside earlier. It would make hauling the extra bag easier. He'd gone out to make one last pass for anything useful. Elaan heard the door open and looked up to find Josh staring open mouthed at her.

"Hey," he said, his eyes drifting to her hair.

"Hey there yourself," she said as her hands deftly braided down the side of her scalp.

"You changed your hair," he said.

"Yep," she said, trying to gauge his reaction. "You don't like it?"

He shrugged. "It's fine," he said. Then he grinned. "I just didn't expect you to go all thug on me."

Did he just say that? She took a deep breath as her fingers worked through her hair. She scrutinized his face. He'd said it, but he clearly hadn't meant any offense. "I'm gonna pretend you didn't just say that, and you're never ever gonna say that to a person of color again. Capiche?"

He said he was sorry, yet he seemed confused as to where he'd misstepped. She finished the plait and then started on the final one. "Listen," she said. "If you were to shave your head to better disguise yourself while on the run, I wouldn't come in and ask why you were going Neo-Nazi or why you were trying to look like a Serbian prison inmate. This is a hairstyle that is easy to maintain when you know you're not going to be able to comb it out and take care of it daily. Maybe thugs wear it for that reason, but that doesn't mean everyone who wears it is a thug."

He nodded. "Seriously," he said, walking over to her. "Sorry. I was just joking around with you. I meant it to be funny. But it wasn't."

She shook her head. "Nope," she said, but then offered him a smile. "But no worries. We're cool."

She took a minute to finish her hair while Josh rifled through the drawers in the room. "You trying to find something in particular?" she asked.

He shook his head. "No, I just want to be sure we don't miss anything. And I didn't look in here earlier because I didn't want to wake you."

"Thanks," she said with a sigh, and then she stood, peeking out the window at the bright sun. She supposed it was time. "So, we just go, start walking?"

He nodded. "After we eat."

* * *

They'd eaten what Elaan considered a "weird" breakfast: canned stew. But they'd wanted a substantive meal before setting out for their walk. Something to keep them fueled up for a while.

They planned to take mainly granola bars, prepacked peanut butter and jelly snack bars, and peanut butter crackers. Elaan had wondered if the people who lived here worked at or perhaps ran some kind of after-school program, because the house had an inordinate amount of these snack things in the storage bins. The dates on the packaging were pretty good. All next year. The wagon was helpful, but they hadn't wanted to be completely reliant on it. So they'd compromised and packed the duffle with mainly light stuff, in case they had to abandon the wagon. The heavier things, a few pull-top cans, and water bottles sat next to the duffel in the wagon. Josh had found a Swiss Army knife, which he reckoned could open a malfunctioning pull-top can in a pinch. The knife could also be useful in other instances.

The plan was to start walking, with an eye toward finding a car. If they got lucky, they'd spot an abandoned vehicle ready to go and get to her mom tonight. But that meant everything had to go perfectly. And given how this trip had gone so far, it seemed unlikely that even two things in a row would go perfectly — let alone *everything.*

They left the farmhouse with Elaan feeling the urge to lock it up, like she would her own house. Only this wasn't her house. It was a temporary stop. Still, it was the first place they'd been since being back uptop that she hadn't been overcome with dread. The train ride, with Willie leering the entire time, had been a ball of stress.

But here with Josh, even though she maybe shouldn't have, she'd felt halfway safe. Now they were leaving. For the unknown. For her mother — a woman who had let her believe she was dead. A woman who could turn Josh into a carrier, if her father was wrong about the type of virus she carried.

She and Josh set out walking in the grass on the side of the road, Josh pulling the wagon alongside him. They hoped they looked inconspicuous enough. They hadn't seen how things worked in the new post-virus world, so they weren't sure how good communication was. Before the world went haywire, wanted people — terrorists, escaped prisoners, "persons of interest" — were broadcast everywhere. But would the government broadcast their pictures in this post-virus world? Could they? Was there still ready power and communication everywhere?

They suspected communication was less frequent, and their main worry would be running into military patrols.

"Josh," she said, as they walked beside a cornfield. It had been harvested already and all that remained were brown, dried-out stalks. "Do you think we should go to my mom?"

He didn't break stride. "Of course," he said. "I promised Lijah I'd take you there."

"I know," she said. "But why? She let me think she was dead. Why does my father think that being with her will be any better than us being on our own? I mean, we survived last night just fine."

He slowed and turned to her. "Elaan," he said, "last night, we got really lucky. But in the future we might not. Squatting is very suspect. Anyone can come back to a house and find us and hurt us for being on their property. Where your mother is, I got the impression, she's supposed to be there. It will be OK for us to be there with her. We won't have to worry about strangers coming around and asking questions. And if she's survived there for months, she knows where to get food, and isn't subsisting on leftover perishables that haven't hit their expiration date."

He sighed and quickened his pace, turning his attention back to the road.

Josh was right, Elaan thought.

They walked straight ahead, following the road. There were almost no cars, which Elaan found strange. It wasn't rush hour, but it was about ten o'clock in the morning and she thought they'd see more vehicles, even in rural Indiana.

"Where do you think people are?"

"Probably staying home, avoiding the virus," Josh said. "We still don't know how bad things are. That place we stayed at was deserted. There was no electricity, no TV, no Internet, not even an old newspaper to help us figure out what's going on now, or even what was going on a month ago."

He was right. It was weird. "How can the world change so quickly, Josh?"

Shaking his head as he stared into the distance, he said, "I don't know. I guess it just does. All the death, all the fear of dying. It changes people. More quickly than you'd expect."

She nodded.

They walked fairly silent for two hours, and Elaan was getting tired. She thought she'd kept in pretty decent shape by working out when she was in the compound, but she wasn't used to this. Not to the steady walking with the sun beating down on them. It wasn't that hot, probably only in the mid-sixties, but they baked under the sun.

They'd seen one house on their walk and decided against checking it out. Josh thought it was unlikely to have a vehicle worth doing anything with. They could see an open garage with a tractor in it. However, the fuel mileage on a tractor had to be bad. Not to mention, it would be very conspicuous, and they were hoping to be stealthy.

They were traveling along what appeared to be an old highway, rather than an interstate. They passed a few businesses and service stations, but they were all closed. They saw a few road signs indicating motorists could find more stores if they turned down a different rural route. But they weren't going to deviate from their route to check for open shops.

Elaan's breathing was heavy and her legs were already sore. "Josh, we should take a break," she said.

He blew out and nodded. "Yeah, you're right. Let's find a place to sit," he said, scanning the area. The grass near the road was fairly high. Whoever was supposed to cut it was probably dead. Up ahead at an intersection with another rural highway, there was gravel on the roadside, instead of tall grass. "Why don't we sit there and take a meal break?"

They settled the wagon, sat on the ground and opened the duffel. They each took two granola bars and a water bottle. They'd refrained from drinking on the journey, thinking it best to conserve water, but as Elaan guzzled nearly half the bottle in just a few seconds, she wondered if they were making a mistake and dehydrating themselves.

The food was good. But so was the rest. It was nice to just not be moving.

"How you holding up?" Josh asked.

"I'm alright, but it's tougher than I expected."

He nodded. "It sounds better in theory, doesn't it? Actually walking a couple hundred miles is — ummm."

"Crappy," she suggested, with a grin.

He shook his head. "Challenging, as my mom used to say. But don't get down. How about, we check out the next house we can spot from the road to see if there's a car?"

She took another swig of water. "Yeah," she said. "And do you want me to take wagon duty? I can pull it, too. No need for you to take it all the time."

Josh eyed the wagon, sipped some water, and shook his head. "It's pretty easy when we walk alongside the road. I've got it for now."

Elaan nodded. They finished their food quickly, and Josh suggested they take an additional ten minutes to rest and go to the bathroom. She envied the ease Josh would have of going near a tree, whereas she'd have to squat strategically to get it done.

After their break, they started up again. By the time they'd walked another two hours, Elaan was distracted and irritable.

Josh smiled. "So, what's going on with you?"

She laughed. "Walking to Illinois. You know, same-old, same-old."

He laughed, too. "Same here," he said. "What a coincidence."

She rolled her eyes, and they walked a moment more in silence, before Josh said, "I meant, what was going on in your head. About your mom. Why did you suddenly decide you didn't want to go?"

Elaan shrugged. "I don't know. I guess I'm a little mad. I just don't understand how she could let me think she was dead. How she could let me mourn her and not tell me. She told Lijah, so why not me?"

"I don't think she did it to hurt you, Elaan. I doubt she thought of it as her telling Lijah and not telling you. She probably would have been happier if Lijah thought she was dead. He might not have hated her so much if he hadn't known the truth."

Elaan shifted her backpack slightly. It was cutting into her shoulder. "I doubt that. He seems intent on hating her just because he feels like it."

Josh shook his head. "I don't think it's as simple as that. I think that if your mother had actually died from the disease, and he took the vaccine to lessen his chances of getting sick, he'd still be unhappy, but he'd mourn. I think he was so angry at your mother because she made him think he needed that vaccine, and she wasn't really dead. If she had really died, if he had a possibility of getting sick, he wouldn't hate her. He wouldn't blame her for her role in his decision to take the vaccine. He's mad because he feels like he's suffered massive consequences for her deception and she's suffered no consequences whatsoever. I also think Lijah feels the way the government did. I mean, your dad said they killed Dayton because he was a threat. But I think they also killed him because they were angry. He started all of this. This whole thing started because he brought this disease here and passed it on to so many people. Only, he didn't die; he was still fine, even though he was responsible for killing millions of people. And nothing had happened to him. Nothing changed for him. He was still healthy and living, even though so many others had suffered."

Elaan breathed out steadily, the backpack weighing more heavily with every step. "So, Lijah hates Mom because he wants revenge. That simple?"

Josh laughed darkly. "I don't think revenge is ever simple, Elaan. But he, on some level, wants justice. Or to feel like there had been some kind of cosmic justice. And the funny thing is that there was cosmic justice, because your mom isn't without suffering. She's off in hiding somewhere. She's without her husband and her children. And everything you've ever told me about her in the compound suggests that she loves you dearly. That she loved being a wife and mother. But all those things are gone for her now. She's alone somewhere, pretending she's not the person she always was, and knowing that she has to spend her life alone because she can make people sick. It's a type of suffering. Only, I don't think Lijah wants to see her perspective. He just sees his own pain."

Elaan stared at him, wondering if he'd somehow managed to earn a psych degree in his first year of college. His analysis of Lijah, of the government seemed so smart, so well thought out. She wondered how he could see things so objectively. She stopped walking, deciding she couldn't think about this and walk, too.

"You alright?" he asked.

Was she? Who knew? Physically, she was fine. She nodded and started walking again. "It's just a lot to think about," she said. They walked in silence for a bit, and Elaan decided to ask the question that was on her mind, but that she wasn't sure she wanted an answer to. "Do you think I'm being like Lijah, that I'm being unfair to her? Seeking vengeance?"

"I didn't say that," Josh said.

"I know you didn't say it," she said, feeling defensive. "That's why I'm asking. I want your opinion. You seem to be more objective about it."

Josh shrugged, adjusting his hand on the wagon he tugged behind them. "You're asking the wrong person," he said. "My mom lied to me, always. From the time I was born until roughly a year ago, almost everything she told me about her job was a lie. She was a spy and I didn't know it. I guess I was mad at the beginning, but eventually I just realized it hadn't been my business, and it had been to protect me, to protect our family. Spies have to conceal their identity from the world, and she couldn't tell a little boy and risk he'd blab to the wrong person. So, eventually I understood it, and I moved on."

They heard the vroom of an engine and turned their heads. Behind them, they saw a pickup truck ambling toward them. They moved further off the road, tugging the wagon into the high grass, to make sure they didn't get hit. The driver, a white man wearing a baseball cap, stared cold-eyed right at them but didn't even slow down, the way passing motorists usually do. He did veer into the other lane a bit to make sure he didn't accidentally hit them, but he seemed hell-bent on not stopping.

Probably was worried they were sick or infected. Elaan sighed. It appeared hitchhiking wasn't an option either. Not that she'd want to get in a car with a stranger after what happened with Willie. Still, she hadn't expected the few cars they saw to just whiz by like that. The driver's face had been angry when he saw them. It was as if he was mad at them for being there. Mad at them for possibly being sick or a danger. Was this what the new world was like? Was it just a big pool of distrust?

Was this a world where those who could get out and about and do things went straight to their destination and stopped for no one?

As Elaan watched the pickup disappear in the distance, Josh said her name. She turned, and noticed he was staring off to the west, where the sun was starting to recede in the sky. "Over there," he said, pointing.

She squinted into the fading light and saw a large cluster of trees. They'd seen trees before, so she didn't know why he'd chosen to point those out. But then she noticed something else, something in the trees. A roof line. It was a house. It was out of the way and hard to spot from the road, so passing motorists or pedestrians wouldn't see it.

"You want to crash for the night?" she asked.

Josh waggled his shoulders. "We've still got a couple of hours of daylight, but let's check the place out. If there's a car and it's deserted, we can crash and drive out tomorrow."

Those were two big IFs, but Elaan was also tired of walking. She wanted one stroke of good luck after everything else.

14

It had taken them half an hour to walk from the road to the house. As they got closer, Elaan grew uneasy. Nothing overwhelming or all-encompassing. Just, in the back of her mind, a little voice saying this wasn't a good idea. The closer they got to the house, the less it appeared deserted.

The grass was trimmed, rather than overgrown, and the windows were fairly clean, rather than dirty like the windows at the previous house.

However, there were no immediate signs of people, either. There were no sounds of people talking, music playing, or anything that might suggest people were home. They stopped a half-dozen or so yards from the front door. Josh set the handle of the wagon down in the grass.

They stood in the yard, examining the house at a distance. Like the place they'd stayed last night, this house was also two levels, but no wraparound porch. Just a set of three steps leading up to the front door, and a small landing with a railing to stand at while you rang the bell. Josh and Elaan stared at the house a long while without speaking. She wondered if he was as apprehensive as she was. Something about the house seemed off, and she wasn't quite ready to go up and knock. And they were definitely knocking or ringing the bell or both. This was not the type of place they dared break into.

Josh didn't move toward the house, and the longer they waited, the more ridiculous waiting seemed. "We've come all the way over here," she said. "We should just go up and knock, get it over with." She started toward the house again, when Josh grabbed her shoulder.

"Wait," he said. "We should put on masks." It took her a moment to remember the N-95 respirator masks. It's what people had been wearing when she'd gone into the SPU. The flimsy masks kept large particles from being inhaled, offering some protection against the airborne Helnoan virus. She reached into her backpack, pulled out a mask, and put it on. By the time she'd finished, Josh had his mask on as well.

"OK," Josh, said. "We'll go together."

He took her hand, and they walked the rest of the distance to the house. When they got to the narrow three steps leading to the door, Josh went first.

That was when the front door opened and the barrel of a shotgun appeared.

"Get back," a male voice called.

A jolt of fear and adrenaline shot through Elaan; she instinctively started to back away. She couldn't see the face that accompanied the shotgun. He was hidden in shadow inside the house.

"We don't want any trouble," Josh said, his voice shaky, as he raised both hands high in the air, as criminals do in police movies. "We just wanted to ask if you had any clean water you could spare."

"Ain't no water here you can't find out in the stream," the gun's owner said. Elaan nodded, and then lowered her head. She didn't want sudden movement to make the man trigger-happy. Though part of her wanted to keep an eye on the gun, in case he started blasting.

"Alright," Josh said, taking a step to the left so his body was now squarely between the shotgun and Elaan. "We don't mean any harm. We're going to leave. We're going to back away just the same as we came. Nothing else."

"Step out from behind him so I can see what you're doing," the man said. Elaan sighed and moved next to Josh. "Good," the man said. "Now, you two leave. Don't come back or I'll shoot you both. Understand?"

Elaan nodded. Her instincts were screaming that she should turn and run, but she forced herself to follow Josh's lead. She kept her eyes on the gun and walked backwards away from the house.

Josh snagged the wagon handle and began pulling it along with them backward. The gunman didn't flinch, but Elaan wondered if it had been a good idea to grab the wagon. While it had a lot of their food and would have been bad to leave, it wasn't worth getting shot over.

"We should move quicker," she whispered.

"I know," Josh said back. "We can turn around in about ten more feet. Shotguns have a much worse range the further you get. We'll turn and run on the count of five," he said. Josh started counting. His pace was slower than Elaan would have liked, but when he hit five, they both turned and sprinted away from the house.

They ran without stopping for several minutes. Josh had taken a bit of an initial lead on Elaan but slowed his pace when he realized he was leaving her behind. When they stopped, they leaned over to catch their breath.

"I can't believe that," Elaan said, her lungs on fire. She leaned forward, trying to take in more air. There didn't seem to be enough fresh air available.

A few labored gasps escaped Josh. "We knew it was a risk." He inhaled a couple more bursts of air and finally said, "Let's just walk the road a bit. We've probably got about an hour more of light. We can figure out a plan for tonight while we walk. I don't think I want to try another house."

Elaan nodded in agreement. "No, not another house."

15

Lijah knew that the daytime was his chance to move, his chance to get to Dahinda. Only, he just wanted to stay put. He'd been through a horrible ordeal yesterday, and he wasn't ready to face the world.

He'd gone through Willie's things after shoving him off the train. The boxes contained everything Lijah had needed to know, including small sealed bags labeled with each stop name. The next stop on the route was the one the inspector had mentioned — the one with the change to a new inspector. That guy had never met Willie, so he'd happily accepted the payment Lijah handed him. It had been too simple, and for a moment, Lijah had considered staying on the train, riding it to wherever.

Only that would have been pushing his luck. He rode on for another half an hour, and jumped from the train as it slowed for a curve. He landed hard, wishing it hadn't had to be this way and feeling a pang of guilt for how he'd shoved Willie off. After getting off the train, Lijah had walked away from the tracks, toward the woods. He'd been a Boy Scout, so he was familiar with trips into the wilderness. His plan had simply been to make camp for the night and figure out his plan in the morning.

Once he was deeper into the wooded area, he

discovered a small cabin that proved to be empty. Back when the world was normal, it would have been someone's idea of roughing it. A cabin in the woods, with only a cot and a couple of blankets. No running water or indoor plumbing, a well and a pump for drinking water, and a wood stove that vented through a pipe in the ceiling.

The cabin was fairly bare. It had a wooden table, two metal folding chairs, the cot and blankets, and an icebox. Inside the few cabinets were a few glasses, plates, and bowls, along with an iron skillet for cooking, but no food.

Last night, Lijah had eaten a bit of the food he'd packed. He'd woken this morning to get some water from the well, taken a leak, and then crawled back in the bed and pulled up the cover. It was nice here. He could live here. He knew which plants were edible, and maybe he'd be able to trap small game for food. He could stay here for a while and not have problems. Here, he'd be away from people who were sick. He'd be safe here, not having to worry about becoming a carrier. He wouldn't have to worry about becoming a killer who spread disease everywhere he went.

And he wouldn't have to see her. He dreaded the prospect of seeing his mother again. After all this time. After she'd set the lie in motion, the one that had changed his life, the one that had led him to think he needed a vaccine, that he needed to take a risk. All because of her. And then she wasn't dead. She wasn't even sick.

"I'm sorry," she'd said when she called him. "I wanted you to know that I'm sorry."

Everything always had to be about her, her truth, and her wants. She wanted to say she was sorry. Well, maybe he had wanted to think that his mother was dead and there had been good reason to try the experimental vaccine. But she hadn't thought about his needs, only her own. She had needed to tell him she was sorry when he hadn't even known she'd done him wrong.

"If they find out," she'd said. "You'll always have a place here with me, where I am."

He didn't want a place with her. He didn't want anything to do with her. He didn't have a place with her. Not after her lies.

He lay there, eyes trained on the ceiling. He wondered whom the cabin belonged to. The owner had probably died in the pandemics, so Lijah could stay here for a while.

Lijah was trying to convince himself that what he was doing was OK. He'd told his father he would get Elaan to their mother, even though he hadn't wanted to go himself. He'd told himself that he would take Elaan there, but he wouldn't stay. But now he was separated from Elaan, and he had to assume that she was safe. That she was still with Josh.

Josh would get her to Dahinda, to their mother. He trusted Josh. He knew Josh wouldn't let Elaan down. And so long as Josh was with his sister, he didn't have to worry. She'd get to their mother without his help. Lijah wouldn't have to see the woman who'd abandoned him, who'd lied to him, who'd expected too much of him and not enough of herself. He'd be fine, and Elaan would be fine.

He told himself this was true. He assured himself that he didn't have to listen to the voice in his head that said he owed it to Elaan to go there. That he owed it to her to show up so she would know he was alright. She hadn't wanted to leave him on the train, and she was probably worried sick about him. She was probably working furiously to get to their mother's to meet up with him, and when he didn't show, she'd assume the worst.

Lijah shook his head. He was making too much of it. He shouldn't feel guilty for wanting to just be alone, for wanting to be free. Going out there, trying to get to Dahinda, meant leaving the safety and seclusion here. It meant he could be exposed to sick people. He could become like Dayton, a murderer, a person who went around spreading disease and pestilence.

Elaan would understand, he told himself. She would understand that he couldn't keep going when it was dangerous for him. She would understand why he didn't want to see their mother. She would understand why staying here was the best thing for him.

Lijah closed his eyes and pulled the blanket over his head. He wasn't leaving right now. He just wasn't. Elaan would understand.

16

Elaan and Josh found an abandoned barn and set up shop for the night. The barn was an odd, random building set a bit off the road. There were no other houses nearby. Just empty fields. It reminded Elaan of the occasional burnt-out building she'd see on their drive to the Outer Banks of North Carolina each summer. Along the side of the two-lane road would just be an old house or a silo, and there'd be nothing else. It was a lonely remnant of some time gone by.

The wooden building was falling apart, and somewhere in the back of Elaan's mind, she wondered if it was a good idea to sleep here. There were a few holes in the ceiling, allowing moonlight in. Elaan and Josh hadn't even had to break in this time. A large hole in the rear wall served as their entry point.

They'd considered sleeping outside under the stars but had heard the distant rumble of thunder and chose this crumbling building instead.

Josh set up their blankets on the ground. To save space, they'd packed one of the fleece blankets from the house last night. They also had the blankets from the SPU. The Mylar blankets looked like thin metal, were lightweight and supposedly warmer than regular blankets because they trapped heat. Josh and Elaan planned to lie next to each other, using all the blankets to try to keep warm.

A week ago, she might have thought the idea of her and Josh alone on a journey romantic. But now she had no such illusions. There was nothing romantic about a cold barn as part of a pit stop for a seven-day walk. She was scared and overwhelmingly anxious. The basics of surviving this trip seemed to trump everything else on her mind.

"I set us up in the corner here," Josh called, startling her.

She turned to see him standing a couple of feet from her and pointing to the southwest corner of the building. The whole barn was probably forty feet by twenty feet, and it had a dirt floor. Josh had laid the blankets down on top of each other. There were no pillows, but it was as cozy as blankets on the ground could look.

They should have searched for sleeping bags when they'd been at that house. Though she wondered if Josh had tried to find sleeping bags and just not mentioned it because he hadn't found any.

"The ground seems to slope just slightly that way," Josh said, as he pointed in the opposite direction of the makeshift bed. "So if it starts to rain, the water should pool away from us."

Elaan nodded. She was glad Josh was here. She was glad he thought of things like the slope of the ground and the rain and all the other stuff that would make their journey easier. But even with him there, she felt lost and alone. They had a long way to go, and they had to figure it out all on their own. That was scary. Scarier than she'd ever anticipated.

"Why don't we eat dinner, and then get some

sleep?" Josh asked.

"Sure." She followed Josh to a spot along the middle of the long wall. It was further away from where they slept, and she supposed it was a good idea to spread out and make use of the space. Besides, she didn't want crumbs to attract vermin to where they were sleeping. Josh had unpacked a can of stew, some granola bars, and bottled water. They sat side by side with their backs to the wall, and dug in. She was actually starving, so she wolfed down her food in a less than ladylike manner, and let out a huge belch after finishing.

She blushed and said, "Excuse me."

Josh laughed and then burped, too. "It's all good," he said.

She smiled. She was quite happy to have eaten, yet she yearned for something else. She wanted something more filling, like a juicy hamburger. She hadn't eaten a hamburger in ages, but she really wanted one right now.

"Our rations are good," Josh said. "I'm glad we decided to bring the extra."

Elaan nodded. She didn't feel like talking. The rations were good, but not so plentiful that she thought she could ask for more. Ten days was a long time. But she wanted more. She wasn't starving anymore, but she wasn't full, either.

"You alright?" Josh asked.

She nodded, and then he frowned. "I'm fine. I'm just tired. It's been a long, long day." Her legs, arms, back, everything ached. Her body had never been a throbbing mass like this before.

"Yeah, I know," Josh said, nodding in agreement. "I didn't think I could ever be this tired. But I am. I was a little afraid I'd fall asleep while talking to you."

Elaan half smiled. She couldn't imagine Josh being anything but attentive while they talked. So, the idea of him falling asleep seemed ludicrous. Yet, maybe he felt just as lost as she did.

"Do you think we'll really be able to do this, Josh? I mean, that guy today, he could've killed us. And Willie?" She shuddered at the memory of his leering eyes.

Josh set his hand on Elaan's. "I know we can do this. We just need to get to your mother, and she'll be able to help us. She'll know where the safe places are. She's been out here for months."

"And if there are no safe places?" Elaan asked.

Josh gently squeezed her hand. "I think there are," he said. "There have to be."

His voice had been firm when he'd spoken. If Josh thought there had to be safe places, then he had to be right. "How far do you think we've traveled today?"

He shrugged. "Probably a little under our target, about twenty miles," he said. "But that's still good. We knew it was going to be a long journey."

Elaan nodded, though his message was a slap in the gut. They needed to go more than ten times that distance, two hundred and ten miles, and they'd only gone twenty. She'd barely survived one day of this. Could she really do ten more just like it?

Josh slid an arm around her. "Don't get down about this. It's a long way. I know. And I'm just as tired as you are. But we can do this. We've got the wagon, the extra supplies, our bravery," he said with a chuckle. "And most importantly, we're going to someplace safe. We just have to get there."

And what if it wasn't? What if her mother wasn't

even there? What if she'd died for real or had to flee? What would they do then? She laid her head on Josh's shoulder. She didn't dare voice her concerns. She couldn't. If he really thought about it, thought about the answers to those questions, he might decide he didn't want to go with her. He might make her go it alone, or demand they try some different journey. She was afraid of what could happen on the journey they expected, but the unknown, a deviation of plan, scared her even more.

"Thank you, Josh," she said, nestled beneath his arm. "Thank you for coming with me. I couldn't do this without you."

He gave her a squeeze. "I'm glad to be here with you. We're going to be OK. We're going to make it there just fine."

17

It must have dropped twenty degrees or more overnight. Elaan awoke feeling as if her face were frozen, even though she was warm and toasty from the collarbone down. Her body was mushed close to Josh's, wrapped beneath the fleece and Mylar blankets.

Josh's arm was around her, adding body heat to the layers of blankets. She smiled, but it faded as she eyed the puddles of water nearby. It had rained overnight.

It was wet and cold. She hated wet and cold. Wet and warm was OK, but wet and cold. Yeck. She tapped Josh's arm and said, "Wake up."

He stirred, rolling over and pulling the blankets with him. Now exposed to the cold, she sat up, and shivered. Josh startled and opened his eyes. "What's going on?"

"It's cold," she said.

Josh sat up, too, the blankets falling away. "You're right," he said. He stared at the muddy floor, and then his gaze focused on their backpacks nestled in the wagon. They'd taken a few empty trash bags from the house to use as rain tarps. Thankfully, they'd been put to good use last night, protecting their things.

"I guess we should put on another layer," Josh said. "But it should warm up during the day. Usually, the shifts between highs and lows are between fifteen to twenty-five degrees. So, it had to be around sixty-five yesterday, so maybe it dropped to fifty, or the upper forties."

Forty degrees was cold. Elaan put on a sweater from her backpack, but she was still cold. She peered out the hole in the side of the barn. It was gray and cloudy outside, like it might rain again. She didn't want to walk in the rain. Even if they had the makeshift rain tarps, that wouldn't be fun. But it wasn't raining at the moment, so maybe it wouldn't start. She sighed.

Josh pulled a sweatshirt from the duffel and put it on. "We should eat and get started for the day," he said.

She nodded. They ate the PB&J along with granola bars and drank some water. Afterward Josh pulled out a map of Illinois and showed it to Elaan. "I think we're here," he said, pointing. "So just inside the Illinois/Indiana border. I've been trying to follow main roads, thinking it will be safer. But we've run into so few people that I don't know that it matters. If we check in for signs often enough, I think we can try a shorter path."

He pointed to the map, showing a few areas that appeared to be forest, or definitely something off-road. Something that could cut off a few miles of walking. Elaan tipped her head to the wagon. "Will that make it?"

"We'll see how far it goes," he said. "The duffel gets lighter with each stop, so we might be able to just carry it, if the wagon can't. But it's a pretty sturdy little thing."

Elaan nodded. "Let's do it," she said.

"The key thing is we'll have to keep on track using just the landscape markers on the map because the smaller roads aren't labeled. If we get off track, we could end up going way off course."

"How far off course?"

Josh grimaced. "Miles. Maybe add a day to our journey."

Not the answer she wanted to hear. "And how much time would we save by going through the woods?"

"Assuming we do it right, we could kill half a day. We might also see an abandoned car if we get a little bit off the main roads."

Elaan bit her lip. Getting there quicker was important. The weather was turning, so the longer it took them to walk, the more cold nights they'd face. A shortcut seemed in order. The downside was bad, but she trusted Josh. She didn't think he'd steer them off course.

"You still want to try it?" he asked tentatively, apparently worried her silence had meant she was second-guessing him.

It hadn't. She smiled big at him and said, "Let's do it. The quicker we get there, the better."

* * *

At first they traveled through dead fields. It smelled of rotting vegetation and the plants were unwieldy, and required more care when walking. The little wagon was pretty sturdy, though, handling the detour with more aplomb than Elaan was mustering. Then they got into the woods, which she realized was worse. Dense trees, undergrowth, spiders and all sorts of insects greeted them. Shouldn't the bugs be dead from the cold? Ick. She hated it.

The good news was threefold. First, there appeared to be a path — not an official one, but one that had clearly been used by travelers in the past. Second, the wagon seemed to be holding up alright. And third, Josh felt confident they were going in the right direction. Despite the density of the woods, they could still find the sun in the sky.

The clouds had dissipated and the sun had come out, making it warmer. They walked at a steady clip, not talking much. It seemed easier to conserve their strength.

Was her mother really going to be so much of a help that it was worth all this? She wanted to find a little house somewhere and stay there until the world finally settled into normal.

"I think that's the edge of the forest up there," Josh said, picking up his pace. "When we come out, look for a pond to the left. That means we're in the right spot. We can take a short break, then follow the road."

Elaan quickened her pace to catch up with Josh. He was focused on the sunlight ahead, indicating the end to the forest. Elaan just wanted to get out of the moist, cool woodlands and into the open again. Something caught her eye. It was metallic; definitely not a color you found in nature. It was the color of something man-made. Curious, she deviated from the path and walked toward it. The grass had grown high enough to touch her waist. The plants were thick and tangled, but she didn't care. There was something familiar and important about the glint of color. As she walked toward it, she realized what it was: a bike.

"Josh," she called and ran toward it. She was so

excited. A bike in the woods! Her heart soared. They'd finally caught that lucky break she'd been hoping for. It wasn't just a regular bike; it was a tandem bike. It was on its side, but the wheels appeared to be in decent shape.

She stopped in front of the bike and stood there smiling, waiting for Josh. This was impossibly wonderful. A bike! A bike they could both use. She scoured the immediate vicinity to see if there was anything else useful, and that was when she screamed. Instinctively she backed away and covered her mouth with her hand.

Josh ran up to her and grabbed her by the shoulders, turning her to him. "What's wrong?"

She pointed to the decomposing couple a few yards away. The two bodies were fairly close to each other, as if they'd died together, lying at the foot of the tree. They weren't just skeletons, but they weren't still bodies, either. Flesh or muck or something dark brown was on top of their bones. But in many places the flesh had been eaten away by animals or insects.

Josh eyed the bodies hesitantly, then reached for the bike. The silvery thread of a spider web shook loose from the frame as Josh lifted it. Elaan stepped back. "You're taking it?" she asked.

"That's why you called me over here, right? For the bike."

Well, yes, that was why she'd called him over, and he was right that it was important. But she'd called him over before she'd seen the bodies, and now taking it made her feel like a grave robber. She knew they needed the bike, but the bodies bothered her. She couldn't help peeking back at the people who were probably its owners. "What about them?" she asked.

"They don't need it anymore," he said, matter-of-factly.

He was right, but she couldn't feel as detached as he did about it. "What do you think happened to them?" she whispered.

Josh's gaze darted quickly to the bodies, before returning to Elaan. "They died. Even if they died of the virus, it can only live for at most, three days after a person dies. And that's in an ideal tropical climate. Last night's cold would've killed anything dangerous. Plus, it seems like they've been dead longer than three days."

Elaan couldn't help eyeing the bodies again, and her breakfast churned in her stomach. Josh had set the bike on the ground so it was upright. The bike had a metal basket on the front. Elaan noticed a water flask near the bodies. There might have been other things at one point, but whatever had been gnawing at the victims probably had also eaten whatever food supplies the couple had, and dragged off anything else useful. She turned away from the bodies, back to Josh. He was surveying the path out of the forest.

"We should carry this," he said. "Can you lift the back end? I don't want to puncture the tires."

Elaan cringed at the sight of the rotting bodies. Then she grabbed the bike under the rear seat and lifted. It was heavier than it looked, but she trudged forward with it, not daring to glance back at the bodies. It took them longer than she would have expected to get back to the path where Josh had left the wagon.

Because the bike's basket was big enough to fit the duffel, they decided to leave the wagon in the woods, a sort of karmic exchange. They put the duffel in the basket, and carried the bike out of the woods in just a few minutes. They set the bike down, and Josh wiped sweat from his brow.

It was sunny now. Despite the rain and chill of last night, the day had turned out to be fairly warm. Josh looked around and frowned. "The pond isn't to our left," he said after a moment. "We're off course."

"How far?"

He shrugged, and scanned the area. Elaan wasn't sure what he hoped to see, but he seemed to have something in mind as his eyes searched the landscape. "I can't tell yet. Nothing is familiar from the map. With the bike, we can make up some time and get to our destination in a third of the time."

There was no one around. But Josh always referred to Dahinda simply as their destination. She supposed it was a good idea, but it also scared her. Was this her new life? Always scared that someone might overhear her, that they might find out where she was going and somehow use that information to hurt her? Or would she end up like that couple back there? Would she and Josh end up rotting bodies on the side of the road, and the people who found them only care about their bike? They'd leave their carcasses to decay by a tree, and steal their stuff. They'd mean nothing to anybody anymore. No one would care what happened to them or what became of them.

"You okay, Elaan?"

She shook her head. "No," she said. "Two people died, and we didn't do anything but steal their bike, Josh. Doesn't that seem wrong to you?"

He wrapped his arms around her. "I know that

seemed harsh," he said. "But that's the world we're in right now. We don't have time to figure out everything that went wrong. We can only deal with the situation at hand and move on. There was nothing we could do for them."

"Bury them," she whispered into his chest. "Something."

Josh rubbed her back. "I know," he said, pausing. "I wish there was something we could do, but we don't have the tools to bury anyone. They shouldn't be contagious, but there are other concerns with moving bodies."

He was right. Always so logical. She didn't want to touch the bodies, but she did feel like they deserved more than what they had gotten, a slow death alone. Well, not quite alone. They had each other, but they were still dead.

"Why don't we say a prayer for them?" Josh suggested.

Elaan pulled away and nodded. "Yeah, I think I'd feel better."

Josh took her hand, bowed his head. "Dear Lord," he began. She bowed her head too, as he continued. "We pray for the souls of those two that have passed. May you take them into your arms and hold them well for their afterlife. May you also give comfort to their families here on earth, and give them strength and courage to continue on without their loved ones. Amen."

Elaan lifted her head. "Thanks," she said. "That was nice. And good, for on the fly."

"It's what the minister said at my mother's funeral."

A funeral for his mother. His mother was gone,

just like … just like she had thought her mother was gone. Only, that had been a lie. Her mother was alive. But Josh hadn't had such good fortune. His mother was gone forever. She squeezed his hand tighter. "I'm sorry," she said. "I know it must be hard for you. I've gotten a reprieve with my mom, news from a soap opera — she's not dead. And you're still without yours."

"A lot of people are without someone they love," he said, releasing her hand. "We need to get on our way."

He turned toward the bike, walked over to it and squatted, feeling the tires. A hint of panic crept into Elaan. The bike was useless without working wheels. "Are they flat?"

"Yeah," he said, but he didn't seem too bothered by it. He unstrapped something from the body of the bike and held it up. It looked like a large syringe. "Portable bike pump," he said, pulling back the plunger. "We can just pump and go. But if there's a puncture from the woods, we can't fix it. So hopefully, they'll inflate."

She watched as he hooked the pump to the bike's tire and began pumping. After a few minutes, he'd filled both tires and given them each a squeeze to assure they were plump enough. "Should be good," Josh said. "I just hope things didn't get rusty."

She nodded. "So, you said the bike could get us there in a third of the time. Is that like two more days?"

"Yeah. If we can do ten miles per hour, which I think is reasonable, for seven hours a day, maybe eight, we'll get there in three days, including today."

Three days. She'd been expecting to walk more

than a week and now, by pushing themselves, they could get there in just a couple more days. Seven hours of biking did seem like a lot. Still, she wanted to see her mother. Josh's mother was dead. He would never see his mother again. But her mother was alive. She'd been thinking about it wrong. She was mad about the deception, but ultimately, her mother was alive. That was more than she should have been able to hope for. A mother who was living and breathing and who she could hug again, see again. She wanted that now. More than anything.

18

Elaan was beginning to feel like everything was running together. They'd biked the remainder of the day they found the bike, and most of yesterday. It had been long and hard but much more efficient than walking.

They'd seen a few more cars on the road; no one stopped and asked what they were doing. No one asked if they needed a hand, either. You'd have thought people would be helpful, or would come together in a crisis. Though, not if the crisis was a virus. The new normal was to stay away from people you didn't know. Anyone they passed seemed intent on staying as far away from them as possible.

Last night, the place they'd stayed had been more like an awning. Something people might have used to store firewood or hay bales. It was only about four feet wide, a piece of tin held up by sticks in a field. They'd woken up cold and with insect bites, but they'd survived another night.

As ambivalent as she was feeling about her mother, she wanted nothing more than to go to her. Her mother's place had to be better than this. She had to have figured out how to set up some type of life, right?

They were pedaling now, and every part of her ached. She hadn't done anything this physically

122

demanding for this long. She just wanted to curl up and lie down in a warm bed with warm food. She wanted home, and nothing said home like Mom. Even a mom who let you believe she was dead.

Elaan tapped Josh, who was peddling in front of her. "Josh, can we take a break?"

He nodded and guided the bike to the side of the road. She dismounted, grabbed a water bottle from the basket, opened it and swallowed down most of the bottle's contents. She sat down on the gravel and put her head between her knees.

"Tired?" he asked.

She nodded and lifted her head. "More exhausted than I've ever been."

Josh had gotten his own water bottle and squatted next her, taking a sip. "I'm pushing too hard," he said. "I'm sorry. We can slow down."

"No," Elaan said. "The days are miserable, but the nights are worse when we have to find some place that turns out crappy. We need to get to my mom, not spend more nights out here," she said waving her arm around at the empty landscape.

She reached down the back of her shirt to scratch a bite she'd gotten.

"No, I'm sorry. We should've tried to find another house," he said.

Elaan shook her head. "After that guy pulled a shotgun on us? No. I don't want to get shot. Too bad your dad didn't pack us a gun." She chuckled, waiting for him to chuckle, too. But he didn't. He just sipped his water and stared at the ground.

"You have a gun?" she asked.

He shrugged. "It's not the most useful. It's a subcompact Beretta Storm." The term didn't mean a whole lot to Elaan.

"Is that a good gun?"

He shrugged. "It's better than nothing," he said. "It shoots nicely, and has a pretty large clip. People tend to like it for conceal and carry, because it's small. Holds fifteen rounds. I have one extra clip."

She had never pegged Josh as a gun enthusiast. But he had grown up in Virginia, and gone to school in Texas, which were two pretty gun-loving states. She sighed and watched him in a new light. "Wait," she said. "So you've had it the whole time? Even when we were on the train? We could have used it to get off the train. Instead of him holding a gun on us, it could have been the other way around. Lijah could be here with us. We wouldn't have had to leave him on that train."

Josh was shaking his head. "When could I have used it on Willie?" he said. "After he pulled the gun on us. He would have shot me if I'd gone for my gun. Before he pulled the gun on us? A preemptive strike? We brandish the weapon, tell him we'll shoot him if he doesn't let us off. And then he lets us off and two seconds later, tells the inspection guy we just got off the train and headed into the mausoleum. We would have been caught immediately. Or were you suggesting I murder him in cold blood?"

"No," she said, feeling guilty for her reaction. "I'm sorry. I shouldn't have said that. It just surprised me, and I'm still upset that we had to leave Lijah. I shouldn't have taken it out on you."

"It's OK," he said. "It's been a rough few days."

They both finished their water. Elaan wanted another bottle, but they didn't have enough for that. They'd gotten lucky and found a well to replenish their supplies yesterday, but biking took a lot of energy and they needed water and food to keep up the pace.

She sighed. "Let's get back on."

"We can rest longer if you want," Josh said.

She did want to, but she wanted to move on more than she wanted to rest. They stood and Elaan wrapped her arms around him. "Thanks for being so nice and understanding. I shouldn't have snapped at you about the gun."

He released her. "It's alright," he said. "We're both stressed."

"Really?" she said. "You don't show it."

"Just 'cause I don't talk about it doesn't mean I don't feel it."

She put a hand on his shoulder. "You can talk to me if you want to. You don't have to keep it all in there," she said as she placed a hand on his chest. "It helps, sometimes if you talk about it."

He shook his head. "I just want to ride," he said. "The physical motion, the fact that I have to concentrate on the road, that helps keep my mind off my worries."

Elaan nodded and smiled back at him, but she did wish he'd confide some of his worries to her. Even though his worries might inspire new worries in her, it would feel better knowing he had worries that were like hers. With little else to say, they mounted the bike and rode off.

* * *

They stopped twice more for a break, and by the time they rolled through a town called Peoria, they were exhausted, and it was five o'clock. They weren't sure they would make it to their destination by nightfall, as they'd hoped. And even if they did, they didn't have a very accurate map. Dahinda was a dot. They weren't going to be able to find the address on their own.

Like most towns they'd passed through, Peoria's streets were pretty deserted. They hadn't talked about it, but it seemed that the death tolls had to be higher than they'd thought. She wondered if the government's desire to eliminate Josh and take her in for further experimentation stemmed from the extreme number of deaths. Something higher than they'd known or understood. The name Scientist Protection Unit suggested it was a place to protect the scientists from the world. But had it been more? Was it a way to protect the human race? A way to make sure at least some people survived? Were things so bad that there was hardly anyone left?

She was feeling a bit dejected, and then Josh said, "Look," pointing up ahead. She craned her neck and saw a gas station: Huck's. She'd seen a few stations with that name, though they didn't have any back at home. The fact that the sign was lit and it appeared to be open made her heart leap.

"Should we stop?" she called.

"Yeah," he said. "We can talk to someone at least, get a better feel of what's going on, and buy some food if he's got any."

"OK," Elaan said, and they rode up a steep incline to the station and parked the bike outside the convenience store part of the station. A neon sign said open, but bars covered the glass doors. Josh walked over and tugged the door handle. It didn't budge.

It was locked. Inside the store, there was food on the shelves. Not full racks of stuff, but definitely enough they could get what they needed. There were chips, candy, snack cakes, canned food, and more. She hated being so close to what they wanted with no way to get it.

Elaan had an urge to smash the glass door and go right in. It was a stupid urge, because it was wrong. And of course, the bars would make smashing the glass useless. That was when they heard a voice.

"What do you want?"

Elaan scanned the area but saw no one besides her and Josh.

"Up here," the voice said.

She and Josh both tipped their heads back and spotted a speaker and a video camera.

"We want to buy some food and water," Josh said to the camera.

The voice from the speaker gave a sigh. "Look through the glass door, write down what you want, and then read me your list. I'll give you the total price, and if you want to pay, tell me. I'll get what you want, and when I let you know, you come around to the side of the building. You'll pay your money through the slot, and I'll give you your groceries through the window."

Josh glanced at Elaan then back up at the camera. He nodded. They walked over to the glass doors and peered inside. "We need water," Josh said. "And I'd like something other than granola bars and those peanut butter and jelly things."

"Me too." As much as she craved something junky and indulgent, the reality of their biking journey weighed on her mind. They needed something that would last. "They've got jerky," she said.

Josh nodded. "There's also a couple of cans of stuff. Beans and wieners, ravioli, that kind of thing."

"It's the kind with the tops you pull off. Let's get two of each." She glanced over at the basket on the front of the bike. "It should just fit, or we can eat it right here. But I want something different."

They took a couple more minutes to decide. Once Josh had finished the list of about a dozen items, including a dessert of shortbread cookies, they waited.

"That will be two hundred dollars," the voice said.

Elaan's eyes widened. "How much?"

"Two hundred dollars," the voice repeated. "If you don't want to pay, get on off the property. Most places are closed because they don't want to get sick. It cost a lot of money to get this setup so I can stay open."

"It's fine," Josh said.

He stepped out of view of the camera and returned a moment later with two hundred-dollar bills. "Where to?" Josh asked.

"Opposite of where you just went," the faceless voice told them.

Josh set out first, with Elaan following behind as he turned the corner of the brick building. They saw a Plexiglas window fixture, the kind Elaan had seen at the post office. It was a thick plastic door with a handle. The door opened vertically. Behind the door was a slot, maybe about two feet deep and two feet wide. On the other side was another Plexiglas door. If it was like the one she'd seen at the post office, only one door could be open at a time. Once Elaan and Josh opened their door, the store owner wouldn't be able to open his until they closed theirs. And vice versa. They wouldn't be able to open their door if the store owner had his open.

Next to the Plexiglas chamber was a mail slot labeled, "Deposit money here."

This man had it all worked out. If he was worried about getting sick, he had less to worry about. He wasn't touching the public at all. The real issue was the Plexiglas chamber. Did he disinfect it after each use, or was it trapped with virus germs?

Josh and Elaan waited silently for a couple of minutes. Then, on the other side of the Plexiglas chamber appeared a rotund man carrying a shotgun in one hand and a brown paper bag in the other. "Put your money in the slot," he said.

"Show us you have everything first," Josh said, sounding firm and no-nonsense. It was tougher than Elaan had ever heard him sound, and she was surprised he pulled it off so well. She'd always viewed him as easygoing and friendly.

The man laughed a little. "I'm not trying to cheat you, but fine." He pulled the items out of the paper sack one by one and held them up to the thick glass. It was hard to make out all the lettering, but it appeared to be everything Josh and Elaan had asked for. On the bright side, the man took cash, rather than gold. So, at least one thing Willie had told them had been wrong. Cash wasn't completely useless.

"You show me the bills before you put 'em in," the man said.

Josh smiled, and held up the bills to the Plexiglas. The man nodded in response, and Josh slipped the money in the deposit slot. After the money was deposited, the man disappeared from view, alarming them slightly. But he came back soon enough and opened his door, putting the groceries in. "Once I close my side," he said, sliding the bag forward, "you can open your side."

The man closed his side. Josh opened their side and grabbed the bag. Elaan said, "Thank you," to the store owner, more out of habit than actual appreciation, though she was glad his store was open.

Josh and Elaan walked over to the bike and put the sack in the basket. They dumped a few empty water bottles in the store's trash can to make room for the new ones.

"Should we eat here?" Elaan asked, as they stood in front of the store.

Josh said no, tipping his head toward the camera. "Let's ride a little bit further, first."

She didn't want to ride anywhere else. She was tired and hungry, but she knew Josh's suggestion was best. "Sure."

19

They rode about a mile down the road and pulled over at a park with a small wooden pavilion that had two picnic tables beneath it. They carried the bike over the gravel pathway so as not the damage the tires, and then rested it against one of the pavilion's posts.

It felt good to sit at a real table. This seemed like a nice area. Elaan could imagine children playing here, mothers sitting at the tables, watching them frolic as they chatted with each other. She could remember normal life, if she tried. But then, of course, reality came slamming back at her. There was no one here.

"Do you think most people are dead?" she asked as Josh handed her a can of pork and beans from the bag.

He just pulled out a bottle of water and set it down.

He must not have heard her. "Josh," she said. "Do you think —"

"I don't think we should speculate about that," Josh said, cutting her off. "Let's just eat our food. It's good stuff. Lots of protein. Let's just enjoy this for right now."

She was surprised at his testiness. He'd been so level during the trip. But maybe this was his fear, the one he didn't want to tell her. That too many people had died. That maybe they weren't getting supplies in the scientist housing because too many people uptop had died. That living down there was going to become a tomb if they were relying on the uptop for help. That the uptop was a goner.

She pulled the tab to open the can of beans and wieners.

"Hey, check it out," Josh said. He smiled as he held out a plastic knife, fork, napkin set. She thought she'd have to scoop out the food with her fingers. "He must have had them lying around still. There are two sets in here. We should keep them, to reuse."

Elaan nodded as she took the packet from him. "Yeah." She smiled. It was nice to have utensils. She ate quietly and quickly. It tasted wonderful. Might it have tasted better hot? Maybe, but it was so much better than granola and those crappy prepackaged PB&Js. The meal lifted her spirits. They ate another granola bar for good measure, then finished off their dinner with shortbread cookies.

Elaan gazed west at the setting sun. "There's no way we're going to get there before nightfall," she said, sighing.

"Yeah, I know," Josh agreed.

"How much further do you want to ride before we search for a place to sleep?"

Josh eyed the horizon and said, "I don't know. Maybe a couple of miles. Hopefully, it won't be so hilly."

"Yeah," she agreed. "No more hills, please." It had taken longer to ride through this area than they'd anticipated. Illinois was known for being flat, but the last twenty or so miles had been up and down hills. Not typical of the rest of the state. Josh thought it was because the river cut through the region. Part of it reminded her of the rolling hills of Virginia that they used to drive through on road trips.

She threw their trash in a can that was about half full and a big, mushy blob. It had been rained on and then dried. As it was a metal mesh can, the ground beneath it was discolored from all the mushy runoff that had settled there. It had clearly been a while since anyone had collected the trash. Another sign of the lack of population.

She sighed and walked over to the bike, where Josh was squatting and staring at the rear tire.

"What's wrong?" she asked.

"It's flat."

"What? How?" She walked over to the bike. The rear tire bulged out from the rim. Josh lifted the bike and pointed to the head of a silver screw sticking out from bottom of the tire.

"We must have run over it right before we got here," he said. "Shit." Josh took a step back, gritting his teeth. "I can't fucking believe this. I thought things were finally starting to go right for us."

"I know," Elaan said softly.

He shook his head and muttered another curse. Josh stomped toward a different pavilion beam and kicked it. His hands were balled into fists and he grunted as he walked toward her, his frustration evident. She was glad to see him finally let it out. Maybe he'd talk to her, open up about what he was feeling. She was about to say something consoling, when she heard the crunch of tires on the gravel. A pickup truck pulled off the road and onto the path to the park. She stared as it rolled up to them slowly.

The old truck's engine rattled and sputtered as it

pulled nearer. The truck was driven by an older black man wearing a baseball cap. He rolled down the window. Josh approached the vehicle to talk to the man, but the driver looked past him, focusing squarely on Elaan.

"Can we help you?" Josh asked.

"Just sit tight where you are you, young man," the older man said. He turned to Elaan. "Are you alright?"

Elaan watched the man. "Umm, me?" she said, pointing to herself and raising an eyebrow.

He nodded.

"Yeah, I'm fine."

The man eyed Josh with suspicion. "I know it's a tough world now, but that don't mean you have to stay with someone who's hitting you. You can get in the car, and I'll take you someplace safe, if you want."

She looked at the man, confused. Josh wouldn't hit her. She wondered what the man was thinking, then realized he may have just seen Josh's one and only airing of frustration during this entire trip.

"I haven't hit her," Josh said, his voice irritated, defensive.

"He hasn't," Elaan said loudly, adamantly, stepping forward. "He's just upset about the bike. It has a flat. We just realized."

The driver looked past them at the bike and shrugged. "But you're alright?" he asked Elaan. He seemed genuinely concerned.

"I'm fine," she said. "But you wouldn't happen to have something that could fix a tire, would you?"

The man peered at her and then Josh. "I actually have some stuff back at my house," he said. "It's in Brimfield, a couple miles up that way." He pointed due west. "I can take you up there, if you want."

"You'd take us to your house and fix our bike?" Josh asked, skeptical.

"I'd take her in a minute," the man said. "She reminds me of my daughter, Natalie. Sweetest girl you ever met, but kept picking the wrong guy. You, I'd take because I don't think she'd go without you."

Josh scoffed, clearly offended. "And you think I'd let her go anywhere alone with you?"

The old man shook his head and gave a slight harrumph. "I don't think you would, because abusers don't like to let their victims out of their sight. So, you wouldn't want to let her go at all."

Josh took a step back and crossed his arms. "I didn't hit her. I wouldn't do that," he told the driver. "And I wouldn't let her go with you because we have no idea who you are. You could be sick. You could have Helnoan. Or you could just be some dirty old man who likes young girls."

The man breathed in deep and took another long look at Josh. "I guess we both have ideas about how bad the other one could be. You tell me you haven't hit her. I'll have to take you at your word. And you can take me at my word. I'm not sick. Not now. I've already been sick. I'm one of those four percent who survived the virus. Three months clean and I been around people since, sick or healthy, and I don't get sick. So I ain't sick, and I don't care if you are." The older man's voice turned wistful as he focused in on Elaan. "I hope she ain't, though. World don't need to lose no one else young and healthy too soon. We done already lost too many people. If you two need help, I'm willing to offer it. But if you don't want my help, I'll go."

"Don't go," Elaan blurted out. She grabbed Josh's arm and said to the man, "Can we talk about it for just a second?"

The older man nodded and turned off the truck's engine.

Elaan and Josh walked back toward the bike and spoke to each other in whispers.

"You're not really considering going with him, are you?" Josh said.

"Yes," said Elaan. "He seems like a nice guy. He just wants to help."

"Boxcar Willie," Josh said. "Did that experience teach you nothing?"

Elaan shook her head. "That man is nothing like Boxcar Willie. He came over here because he thought you were going to hurt me."

"Have you thought that maybe he just used that as an excuse to get you to trust him? Given how few people we've seen, maybe he figures he can just take us to his house, kill me, and do God knows what to you."

Elaan understood what he was saying. Logically speaking, she should probably agree with him. But her gut told her to trust this guy. Willie instantly and immediately gave her a terrifying vibe. This guy didn't. She believed him when he said he wanted to help. She didn't think he'd hurt them. "Let's go," she said. "Just long enough to fix the bike and then we'll leave."

"I don't like this, Elaan," he said.

She glanced back at the man. "Come on, trust me. We'll stick together and leave as soon as the bike is fixed." Josh was still gritting his teeth. "Come on, biking was bad, but walking was worse. We're so close, and if we can just have the bike for a bit more, we'll get there faster. And," she paused, not sure she wanted to admit her fear. "If for some reason, my mom isn't there, we may need a backup plan. We may need to go somewhere else. If we can fix the bike, rather than ditch it, it would be better."

Josh bit his lip as he scrutinized the man in the truck. "This is a bad idea, Elaan," he said. "We don't know anything about him."

Josh wasn't budging. She wasn't sure what to say. She closed her eyes and rubbed her temples. "Josh," she said. "This is the first place in a long while where we've seen anything open. And this guy stopped for us, too. Maybe this area is different. Maybe there are more people around, and maybe this is the kind of place with heavy patrols after dark. I don't want to be out at night when we don't know much about this place. Let's just get a ride with him get the bike fixed, and get on the road."

He didn't speak, his face frozen with a scowl, as he seemed to ponder her words. Finally, he said, "Fine. But we stick together. We don't separate at all while we're with this guy."

"I promise," she said, beaming. "I won't leave your side."

Elaan started toward the truck, but Josh put out a hand to stop her. "I'll talk to him, alright?"

She thought the driver would prefer to hear the news from her, but the fact that Josh had agreed meant she should probably defer to him.

Josh walked half the distance to the truck and spoke loudly. "We've thought it over and if you're still offering, we'd be glad to accept your help. We just need to make sure we've got everything."

The old man leaned out the window and spit into

the dirt. "That'll be fine," he said. "You can put the bike in the truck bed when you're ready, and then you two can ride up front with me." The man spoke to Elaan. "My name is Lee. Lee Payton."

"I'm Priya," Elaan called out. Even though she thought Lee was harmless, she thought it was better to use her fake name.

"Good to meet you," Lee said.

Josh didn't offer a name, choosing to simply walk back to the picnic table and start rummaging in his backpack. Elaan was pretty sure they'd packed everything, but then she saw Josh pull a gun from the bottom of the pack and move it to the pack's outside zipper pocket. She looked back to see if Lee had noticed. He was looking in their direction, but Josh's back was to him, so she doubt he'd seen.

She edged closer to Josh and whispered, "You think we'll need that?"

"I don't trust him," he said, as he turned and smiled at Lee. Josh slung the pack over his back, walked over to the bike, and grabbed the handlebars. Elaan helped Josh carry the bike to the truck, but then Lee hopped out and helped Josh lift the bike up into the truck bed.

After the guys had finished maneuvering the bike in, Lee went over to the driver's side door and held it open for Elaan. "You can take the middle seat and your friend, who didn't give his name and thinks it's a good idea for ladies to carry a bike when able-bodied men are nearby, can ride in the passenger's seat."

Josh gave Lee a cold stare but headed toward the passenger door. Elaan got in, sliding past the steering wheel and stopping in the center. Then Lee got in and started the car. Elaan found a lap belt and buckled it.

Josh strapped himself in as well. Like Elaan, he'd put his backpack in his lap, but Josh's hand rested firmly on the opening of the front pocket. Elaan tried not to stare.

She smiled at the old man, who backed the vehicle up and turned west. At least they were heading in the right direction, even if Josh thought it was with the wrong man.

20

Lee's definition of a couple of miles up the road was different from everyone else's. Or perhaps just loose language. The good news was they were heading due west, the direction they needed to go. Eventually, they turned right down a long driveway and stopped at a little brick house with an attached garage. About fifty yards to the right of the house was a barn.

"This is it," Lee said, climbing out of the pickup. "Come on in the house for a minute, first."

Josh gave her an "I told you so" look. Lee was standing at the open driver's side door waiting for her. She glanced up at the house. It was a cute two-story, colonial. It didn't seem like the lair of a depraved man, but Josh had spooked her a bit by mentioning Willie. Her gut said Lee was fine, but she was on alert as she slid across the seat and hopped out.

Lee shuffled to the front door, and Elaan followed slowly, waiting for Josh to catch up. He'd said they should stay together. After a moment, he was beside her, threading his fingers through hers. His backpack hung from his shoulder. They stood on the steps to the front door, behind Lee as the old man searched for his key. Once he found it, Lee opened the door, let them in, and flicked a switch turning on the lights.

Elaan's insides sang. Power. He had power. It seemed so glorious to have lights on. She wondered if Lee was actually the norm, rather than the nothingness they had seen in their walk and bike ride. Were there other people living with power, in homes, happy people with cars who'd survived and were willing to help?

Lee shuffled in and set the baseball cap he'd been wearing on a hook near the door. Without the hat, you could see Lee's gray hair and a bald spot on the top of his head.

"Come on in," he said, and he waived them inside. Elaan walked over to the middle of the living room, standing in front of a sofa, but not sitting. The room had a fireplace on the rear wall, and on the mantle were several photos. Her eyes gravitated toward a large picture of a girl on the mantle. The girl was older, but she bore a striking resemblance to Elaan.

Without meaning to, Elaan took a step toward the picture.

"That's my daughter, Natalie," Lee said, from behind her. "You favor her. That's why I stopped when I saw you today. I wanted to make sure you were alright."

Elaan turned back to Lee and smiled. He seemed sincere. She could tell he didn't mean them harm, but after seeing the picture of his daughter, she started to wonder if Josh was right about Lee's interest in her being too much.

"I'm fine," Elaan said reassuringly. She turned to Josh. "Ethan was just upset about the bike. He wouldn't hurt me. Ever."

Lee shrugged, but he gave Josh a hard stare, as if he still thought ill of him.

"You were going to help us fix our tire?" Josh prompted. "So we could get on our way."

Lee nodded. "Yeah. I'll help you fix it," he said, his tone clipped, and then he sat down in the armchair. "But I wanted to offer you both a place to stay for tonight. Under the Martial Law, you're not supposed to be out after dark, and I can't imagine you'll get where you're going in the next twenty minutes."

Elaan turned to Josh. A place to stay. After waking up covered in bites, a real place to stay, a place with electricity and a fireplace and indoor plumbing, would be like heaven. Josh, who had been watching her, turned toward Lee when she tried to catch his eye. "You've already done so much for us," Josh said. "I don't think we should impose on you further."

Elaan couldn't help but frown. Josh didn't want to stay. He had gotten a completely different vibe from Lee than she had, and now he wanted to sleep in the weeds rather than in a house with this man. She wasn't sure she agreed with that.

Lee gave Josh a stern gaze. "Don't let pride stop you from doing what's best for your girl," he said. "A real man would accept the help of a kind stranger, make sure his gal is taken care of."

Lee turned to Elaan. "How long you two been dating?"

Elaan was surprised that Lee asked. And she didn't have a ready answer. Josh chimed in with an answer that almost made her jaw drop.

"We're married," Josh said.

Elaan forced her mouth to stay shut and tried to keep a neutral expression. She wasn't sure why Josh said that, but she didn't want to contradict him either.

Lee sat back in the chair, his eyes narrowing. "You

two seem awfully young to be married."

"We are," Josh said. "She's eighteen and I'm nineteen, but we knew we wanted to be together, and with so many people being sick, it didn't seem like there was any reason to wait."

Lee still seemed suspicious, but he just said, "Suppose not." The older man stood, with effort. Lee seemed old fashioned but his face didn't look that old. However, he moved wearily, like he was tired or injured. She wondered if that was a leftover effect from surviving the Helnoan virus. Did anyone ever fully recover? "The tools we need to fix your bike are in the garage. I'm going to go set up so we can patch the tire — find everything we need. Why don't you two decide if you want to stay while I do that? The guest room's upstairs. Second door on the right."

Lee walked past them and out the front door. This time he didn't lock it.

Josh watched the door for a moment or two after Lee left, then turned to Elaan and whispered. "There's something weird about this guy." He set his backpack down on the sofa, checked for signs of Lee returning, and took out the pistol. He flipped a small lever on it, pulled back the top part, making a loud metal click, then flipped the lever again and put the gun back in the pocket.

"What did you do?" she asked.

"I chambered a round," he said.

"What does that mean?"

He peeked to make sure Lee hadn't returned. "To fire a gun, a semiautomatic gun, you have to have a bullet in the chamber. Revolvers have six chambers, six bullets. Once you shoot, you spin to a new chamber to fire. This gun," he said, pointing to the backpack, "feeds automatically after you chamber the first bullet. I had the safety on, and no round chambered. That prevents a misfire. But since we may need it, I chambered a round. Now all you have to do is take the safety off and you can fire it."

Elaan sighed. She hadn't planned on a gun lesson. "We have to decide whether to stay," she said. She pointed at the backpack pocket where he'd put the gun. "So, I'm guessing your vote is no."

Josh sighed, peeking at the doorway again. "Listen," he whispered. "I know how rough last night was, and I don't want a repeat. This house is tons better than anything else we've seen, but I don't know. He seems fixated on you and dislikes me a lot."

Elaan shook her head. "He just got the wrong impression," she said. "For some reason, he thought you were going to hit me. We can convince him of what a nice guy Ethan is."

Josh rolled his eyes. "And next stranger we meet, let's be Jake and Emma. We don't know what happened with Willie, and we certainly don't want him to tell people we were using the names Priya and Ethan."

Josh made a good point. Elaan nodded. She'd gone with Priya because it was easy to remember. But what if Willie had told people at the next checkpoint about them? And what if he'd hurt Lijah? She shuddered as she thought of her brother. She'd been decently successful at putting Lijah's predicament out of her mind. At pretending she was confident of his safety. But at moments like this, her fear that something awful had happened to him returned.

She had to focus on the moment, not Lijah. She peeked at the door again. "He's weird but harmless. I think we should stay."

Josh sighed. "Fine, we'll tell him we'll stay," he said. "But all bets are off if he tries anything weird in the next hour. Also, we make sure we patch the bike tonight, and we sleep with a chair pressed against the door, and our friend," he pointed to the outer pocket of his bag, "is on the nightstand and ready for action, OK?"

Elaan nodded. She turned toward the door, so they could catch up with Lee in the garage, but she stopped, as one last thing popped into her mind. "Why did you tell him we were married?"

Josh flushed. "I'm sorry I didn't ask first," he said. "But you looked like Christmas had come early when he offered us a room. He seems so old fashioned and hostile toward me, I knew he'd tell us to stay in separate rooms if I said you were my girlfriend. We promised we'd stay together. I just wanted to make sure that happened."

"Good thinking," she admitted, admiring his read of the situation. For good measure, she added, "Hubby."

He gave her a good-natured scowl. "OK, wifey."

The two of them headed outside and found Lee where he said he'd be: inside the garage. Lee helped Josh lift the bike out of the truck and they took it inside. The repair seemed fairly easy with the tools Lee had. With a flat-edged tool, he removed the tire from the bike, then pulled the screw out, added some type of goo to the hole, and placed a little plastic patch over the spot.

"Should be set in a half an hour," Lee said. "You'll just have to pump it. You can leave and deal with the patrols, or you can stay. Have you decided?"

Josh nodded. "Just because the world's gone bad doesn't mean all people have. You've offered us hospitality, and we'd be glad to accept."

Lee nodded, and they all walked to the house and settled in the living room. Josh and Elaan perched themselves on the sofa this time, trying to be gracious recipients of Lee's hospitality. Lee offered to get them some water, but Josh declined for the both of them.

Despite Josh's misgivings, he smiled affably at Lee and tried to be friendly as Ethan. Josh adapted well to the lie he'd told. He sat uncommonly close to Elaan on the sofa and had threaded his fingers through hers.

"Lee," Josh said, respectfully. "We've been riding from Ohio, and we haven't seen a lot of people. We're trying to get a sense of what's been going on. It just wasn't like this in Ohio. Are there usually so few people, so few things open?"

Lee watched Josh, doubt in his countenance. "Ohio is drastically different from here?" he said.

"It's hard to say," Elaan said. "We tried not to go out much. We didn't want to get sick."

Lee nodded, his expression easing, as if her answer had made perfect sense. "Yeah, people around here don't go out much either."

"Don't they?" Elaan said, hoping he'd keep talking.

"No," he said. "I'm probably more of a renegade. Always had been. May — my wife — always said I didn't know when to stop, that I just kept going 'til I got what I wanted." He chuckled at the memory. "She was a good woman. We were married for thirty years."

Elaan tried to guess his age. He was older, but she hadn't expected him to say he'd been married for thirty years.

"You married young, like us?" Josh suggested.

Lee nodded. "Got married at twenty," he said. "She died this spring. We both got Helnoan, but May didn't make it. And then Natalie, my daughter, I don't know where she is. I always hold out hope she's OK, but with the way things are, there's no way to know."

Outside, the sky was darkening. "Sometimes it's hard to get them to come for the dead," he said in a low voice. "May had gotten sick first, and I'd nursed her through it, or tried to. When she died, I called and asked them to come, but I never heard back. I took the backhoe and dug a hole. Buried her over yonder, near the tree line. Then I got sick, could barely do anything for myself. But somehow I made it."

Elaan turned toward the window, thinking of the man struggling with his wife's corpse. "I'm so sorry," she said. "That must have been hard for you."

"Life is hard," he said, unflinching. "You just have to go with it."

"When was the last time you saw your daughter?" Elaan asked. "Do you think she'll come back?"

Lee smiled wistfully at that. "Natalie," he said. "I saw her in October of last year, before the virus had hit the US, really. But I talked to her in February. She was such a good girl, such a sweet girl. Always calling to check on us, always kind to us. She'd have been a nurse, too. She was studying that at the U of I, when she married that Ray fellow. He convinced her to drop out. Said she could transfer to a new school, somewhere cheaper, but then he came up with some reason why it made more sense for her to take a semester off. Convinced her to move to Chicago with him. Convinced her that being his wife was the most important thing."

He shook his head and grimaced. "She had a bruise on her cheek and she said she fell. Always some damned fall. I told her it was OK, that she didn't have to stay, and she kept lying to me that Ray hadn't done anything, that Ray was a good man. But I knew. Her mother knew, too. But May said if we kept pushing, she wouldn't talk to us at all. I wanted her to leave him. I wanted her to see what he was." Lee's eyes were focused on some point in the distance, anger simmering beneath the surface. "But she didn't want to see. She didn't want to believe, and I sometimes wonder if I did something wrong, so she didn't realize what he was doing was bad. 'Not everyone is like you, Daddy,' she used to tell me. 'No boy will ever be good enough to you, Daddy.' That's what she'd say. But someone who loved her, truly loved her, would've been good enough. Still, last I saw her was almost a year ago. She called in February and said she and Ray were going out west, to stay with his uncle in Arizona. But I ain't heard from her since."

Elaan took in a small breath. His hostility toward Josh made more sense now. Poor Natalie.

"It was about a month after the virus really took hold hard," Lee said. "And since then, I just been hoping to hear from her. May got sick just after Natalie called. She don't even know her mother died. May and I had gone into town to get some supplies to tide us over. She wanted mason jars for canning. She had some, but she got more. And I had gotten some ammunition for my guns. That was hard to get. A lot of gun stores were running low, but I been a customer for thirty years and Johnny had stashed me some ammo, when I called and told him I'd pay double. We came home, thinking we were good, thinking May and I were set to ride this thing out for a while. But a few days after that trip, May got the fever."

He shuddered at the memory. "Eventually, I got a fever, too," he said, his voice low again. "I took the best precautions I could, wearing a mask, wearing gloves. It seemed to have worked. Even though May had passed, I was in pretty good shape, I thought. Then it hit. The fever, the bleeding, the vomiting. Every part of you hurts when you get that disease." He closed his eyes, breathed out, and then opened them. "But enough about me and my misery. Why are you two riding through Illinois? Where you headed?"

Josh leaned forward and said, "The Quad cities. Both our folks died, and we have relatives up that way. At least we had 'em. No telling if they're there now, but there was nothing left for us back where we were. We thought maybe it was safer out here where there are fewer people."

Lee shrugged. "Well, there are fewer people, but I can't say it's tons safer. Some people try to come out here and steal. I lock all the doors and sleep with my Derringer just in case."

Josh nodded solemnly, and Elaan sat still and silent. She hadn't expected this. She'd thought that they were on a quiet, sleepy farm, not a place rife with crime.

"Do people try to break in often," Elaan asked.

Lee shook his head. "Not often, but enough that it's something I'm prepared for." Lee smiled at Elaan. "Don't worry, Priya. If I hear anything overnight, I'll come out shooting. I do recommend the two of you stay in your room, though, as I'll be shooting first and asking questions later." He chuckled at his little joke, and Elaan forced a smile.

"We'll stay put," Josh said. He paused, then started another question. "We've been trying to carry supplies with us, but thought in a real emergency, maybe we'd be able to stop and buy things. Frankly, until we hit this town, most of the stores were closed. If everything is closed like that, how do people get things?"

Lee nestled back in his chair. "There are stores open. They just do business differently. They have a special booth set up. Some of them have people in them. Others have a computer. You can give the person your list or type it in. They see if they have everything, and once you pay, your items get delivered at another booth. It keeps contact down. The real problem is with so many people dying, there just aren't enough supplies. And people try to avoid going out as much as possible. No need to expose yourself to the virus if you don't have to."

Elaan nodded.

"So Ohio was different?" Lee asked. "People going out all the time."

Josh shrugged. "Not all the time, but I think more often than here."

"Where's about in Ohio?"

"Cleveland," Josh said, and Elaan marveled at his ability to think on his feet, to lie quickly and adeptly without seeming like it was a lie. Or perhaps it wasn't him thinking on his feet. Perhaps he had thought through their entire story while they were on the road. Perhaps he'd been prepared, whereas Elaan had just been moving through their situation, realizing too late she'd have to answer questions like these.

"Seems odd that they're so cavalier," Lee said. "So, why'd you leave?"

"We'd been holed up with a couple of immunes. They'd gone to get us supplies," he said. "But they decided to leave, to go back out East, where they were from."

Lee stared. "Out East seems like it would be worse off than Ohio. A lot of people, fewer resources."

"It was central Virginia, so a little more rural than the bigger cities," Josh said. He had an earnest expression on his face and seemed to be trying to look as nonthreatening as he could. She'd always thought Josh knew how to interact with people, and she got the impression Lee was softening toward him.

Josh spoke again. "Our friends only had cell phones, and the service died a few months ago. Do cell towers still work around here? Or is it just landlines?"

Lee shook his head. "Depends," he said. "They don't repair the cell towers if they're broken or have a problem. If you have service, you do. If you don't, you don't. The landlines are a bit better. The government telephone numbers at least seem to ring if you dial 'em. That doesn't mean a live person will answer, but they ring. A lot of the numbers are disconnected. If something goes wrong with the line, they don't send people out to fix it. There aren't enough people."

Spotty phone service, people scared. She'd missed so much living in the SPU. Her life there had been easy. Up here, people were dying or afraid of dying. "How many people do you think have died?" she asked. "Does anyone report numbers, maybe on the news?"

Lee narrowed his eyes at her. "Ain't no news. Ain't been no news in weeks. Them people who broadcast the TV don't air nothing now. Most I can get is static. Y'all got more in Cleveland?"

"The house we were in lost power," Josh said. He wrapped an arm around Elaan. "It was pretty harsh for us, and we just thought we'd do better leaving there, do better with family."

Lee sighed, nodded. "Well, I hope y'all get what you're looking for, that your folks ain't dead, that you haven't traded Cleveland's harsh winter for Iowa's. If I were you, I'd have headed for Virginia where it's warmer. Winter is coming and it will be cold, snowy, and frozen."

Elaan hadn't thought of it like that. She knew winter was coming and they needed to get to Dahinda, sooner rather than later, but she hadn't thought of the harsh winter's effect on them once they arrived. If the house her mother was at had no electricity, then it would be tough. Though Lee had electricity and running water.

"How are you going to survive?" Elaan asked, before she could stop herself.

He smiled. "This is the country, Priya," he said. "The garden had been planted before May got sick. After I got well, I used all the mason jars she had to can up the stuff that had grown. I was able to grow some more. It's not the most, but it's a decent start. I also plan to hunt. Wild turkeys run right through my front yard. And deer. I see deer all the time. I can survive on canned vegetables and well water, and the occasional animal I hunt."

Gee, he was so self-sufficient. She couldn't

imagine being that way. But was she going to have to learn all this stuff? Would she need all that to survive? Josh glanced out the window. Elaan followed his gaze, noting it was dark now. It had to be after eight o'clock.

"It's getting late," Lee said. "Let me show you your room."

He stood and walked past them toward the stairs. Elaan and Josh followed behind him, up the steps to a little landing. In front of them was a few feet of space and then two doors. Lee walked over and opened the door on the left. "Bathroom," he said. Then he opened the door to the right. Inside was a room with a queen-size bed and not much else. "Guest room."

Lee turned around and pointed ahead. Josh and Elaan turned too, noticing another door on the other side of the stairwell. "That's Natalie's room," he said. "Don't go in there."

Elaan and Josh nodded. "My room is downstairs, just past the kitchen," he said. "It's an addition we did to the back of the house. Has its own fireplace, too. I don't normally heat the whole house because of that. It should be warm enough up here, but there's a linen closet in the bathroom. You'll find clean sheets and extra blankets in there."

Lee stepped toward the stairs, and Josh and Elaan moved out of the way. "I'm gonna head to bed now," he said. "And please stay put in the house until I come tell you I'm up. I'm a light sleeper. I don't want to be startled awake and forget I have guests."

"I understand," Josh said. "We'll probably just brush our teeth and stuff, and then head to bed."

Lee nodded.

"Thank you," Elaan said. "Thank you again for your hospitality."

Lee smiled, and put a hand on Elaan's shoulder. "Of course," he said. "I would like to think that if Natty was in trouble out there, that someone would do the same for her, you know. That someone would show her kindness when she needed it. At least I hope someone will. They used to talk about paying it forward. I guess this is me doing that. Hopefully, Natty is alright and don't need no help. But if she does, I hope someone gives it."

21

Things felt almost normal as they got ready for bed that night. A real house with running water and electricity. They brushed their teeth at a sink instead of dumping a capful of bottled water over their toothbrush bristles.

Elaan and Josh washed their faces and then went to the bedroom Lee had assigned them. They made the bed and lay down together. The situation reminded Elaan of a few nights ago, but it was different this time. This place seemed safer than that one. And this time, Josh had told the occupant that they were married. She was attracted to Josh and they were certainly more than friends, but they also weren't intimate yet.

She startled at that thought. Yet.

Before she could ruminate on it more, Josh whispered, "In the morning you should ask Lee if it's alright for you to take a shower. I thought about it tonight, but didn't want to do it without asking. If he says it's alright, we'll get clean, have some breakfast, and head out. I think it's only about twenty miles, so we should be able to get there in plenty of time to find your mom before it gets dark."

Elaan nodded, then yawned. "That sounds like a good idea."

Josh laughed. "You tired?"

"Exhausted," she said. "I thought it would get easier as the days went on, but I still hurt everywhere. I don't think people are meant to bike so much each day."

"I don't think so either. I'm exhausted, too," he admitted.

Elaan rested her head on Josh's shoulder and closed her eyes, thinking how nice it was to lie close like this. Just then, he pulled away, and said, "We should probably get some sleep."

He turned off the light and then climbed back into bed.

She lay there next to him, her mind still full of thoughts, still too busy for sleep. "Josh," Elaan said, her voice soft. "Are you ... Do you?" She paused, feeling timid, feeling stupid asking this question. "Never mind."

"No, don't do that," he said. "We're living in a world with a dangerous virus, where we are some of the few people left. So don't do that. Don't start to ask me something and then stop. You can ask me anything. I'll answer."

Anything. Hmm. "I didn't mean to just stop mid-question," she said. "It's just. Y'know when you worry you're going to make a fool of yourself?"

"There's nothing you could say that would make me think you were anything less than wonderful."

Elaan blushed at the compliment. "See, you do that, and then you —"

"I what?"

"You just stop," she said. "You said you didn't want to think of me the way you thought of Lijah, but then you lay in that bed next to me and you completely avoided me."

He pulled her closer to him, and she breathed out, the warmth of him sending warm tingles through her, making her forget she doubted his affection, that he could feel anything other than what he did.

"I know," he said. "I stop. I pull away, because I just don't want to mess things up."

"You couldn't mess things up."

He chuckled. "I don't know about that," he said. "We're here, together, because Lijah told us to get off the train. Because he stayed to protect you. And we're running from a government who wants me dead and you for experiments. It's stressful for you, and physically, it's hard. I just don't want to push you. I just don't want you to feel like I'm trying to take advantage in a time of stress in your life. I don't want to mess things up between us, Elaan. I don't want to push you."

"You're not pushing me," she said, turning toward him.

"I know," he said. "I've known for a long time that I'm falling in love with you. And Lijah was against it, so I tried so hard to push you away. And now that he's gone, even though he said he was OK with us, I know he'll hate me if I hurt you, if I push too quickly, so I'm trying to be good. It's not because I don't like you, Elaan. It's because of how much I do like you that I stop."

"You don't have to be good," she said, kissing him.

*　*　*

Elaan was awakened by the sound of knocking on their bedroom door. It was Lee, saying he was up, and they could wander around without worrying he'd shoot them. "Thanks," Josh called out.

Josh had one arm wrapped around Elaan, and when she opened her eyes, he leaned in and kissed her. "Good morning," he said.

She smiled groggily. "Good morning," she said, then closed her eyes again. "I don't want to get up."

Josh chuckled. "Then sleep a little bit longer, but we should get on the road sooner rather than later."

Elaan opened her eyes again, and without Josh leaning in to kiss her, there was no protection from the glare of the sun streaming through the window. She sighed and slid over just a little to get the sun out of her eyes. Josh didn't move.

She whispered, "What're you thinking about?"

He sighed. "Just today. It's the big day: the end of our journey. I'm just thinking about that."

She sat up. "It will be good," she said, though she wasn't entirely sure she believed it. "I mean, my mom will know what to do. She'll have this figured out, the way Lee does. I mean, Lee gives me hope." As she said it, she realized it was true. If Lee had figured out how to survive in this weird new world, and he still had electricity and his well, then maybe her mother was doing the same.

Josh nodded unenthusiastically and sat up. "We should find out from Lee if it's alright to run the shower."

They both climbed out of bed and threw on last night's clothes so they'd be presentable. They wandered downstairs and found Lee in the kitchen. He was sipping a cup of hot tea. Elaan asked if it was alright for them to shower, and Lee said that was fine, but to be short because he didn't want to tax his well.

They went upstairs, took turns showering, then got

dressed and headed back down to the kitchen. Lee was still in there, reading a Bible. He offered them some cucumbers and tomatoes he'd canned. Thankful for something different, they gladly accepted and ate at the table with the old man. He seemed more amiable this morning.

After half an hour, Josh stood and thanked Lee for his hospitality.

"Just treat her right, and I'll be happy."

Lee walked them out, and Josh asked for directions to Iowa. Lee told them to stay on Rte. 150 and then suggested taking some other highway, but Elaan tuned out. Josh was just trying to make Lee feel needed. They were going to Dahinda, and Josh knew the way. Whatever Lee was telling them didn't matter.

"Travel safely," Lee said as they rode off. From his lips to God's ears, Elaan thought.

22

The bike ride from Lee's house to Dahinda had taken a little over an hour and had been uneventful. It was almost too easy, compared to the rest of their journey. But maybe that was good. Maybe their fortune was changing. Maybe things were working out for the better.

The little road sign that said "Welcome to Dahinda" was small and blue. They rode a few minutes more, passing three streets that didn't have signs. Then they saw a sign that said "Leaving Dahinda."

"Fuck!" Josh said. It was exactly what she was thinking.

The entire town had taken them literally five minutes to blow through on a bike, and there didn't appear to be anything in it.

"Do you have the address?" Josh asked.

"Yeah," she called out, thinking back to the letters from her father. "It's 4801 Crystal Circle."

He shook his head. "I have no idea where that is."

"Me neither," said Elaan. "Except Lijah said it's a lake community. I don't see a lake yet."

As far as she could see down Rte. 150, there were no cars, no people. They had passed a couple of streets that shot off to the right. "Let's go back and explore the side roads. This address has to be down one of these roads."

The two of them biked a long way down two different roads, exploring houses, hoping to find this supposed lake, and came up empty. After an hour, they returned to the final road that jutted off the main road. It was the first road past the Welcome to Dahinda sign. They turned down it, riding on a straightaway for a bit. Then they came to a fork in the road and decided to turn right. After another mile, they saw a sign that said "Welcome to the Maple Leaf Lake Community."

Elaan smiled, her heart thumping with joy. This had to be it.

A little ways back from the sign was a building labeled "Maple Leaf Visitor's Center."

"Josh, we should stop there," Elaan said. "I bet they'll have a map."

"Alright," he said and they pulled over and dismounted at the building. Josh walked to the metal doors and pulled the handle. Of course, it was locked.

Elaan sighed as she joined him. "So, what now?" she asked.

Josh eyed the locked doors and then took a step back to survey the building. It was single-story with beige aluminum siding. It was deeper than it was wide, a big long rectangle. The front part didn't have any windows.

"Let's check around back, see if there's another door." Josh walked the bike around with them. A couple of narrow windows adorned the building's long side. Peeking in, they only saw a typical office. In the rear corner of the building, there were two double doors. The doors should have been locked. But the lock appeared broken. Josh smiled and pulled on the door. It opened. Elaan took a step forward to go in, but Josh tugged her back. He shook his head and motioned her to stay there, as he went in.

She grabbed the door, holding it open and watching as Josh entered the darkened building. He hadn't pulled out his flashlight, so he'd only have slivers of light from the open door. She looked in but couldn't see him. He was gone a few minutes, and Elaan started to worry. She was about to call his name, when he emerged from the darkened hallway carrying something. As he got closer to her, she realized it was a brochure.

He handed it to her and spoke. "It's just your typical visitor center — brochures and stuff. Perhaps someone had broken in to steal food or money. A lot of the stuff was overturned, but I found that."

Elaan looked at the folded brochure in her hand. It was glossy paper, with the words "Maple Leaf Lake Community." Josh stood next to her so they could read the brochure together.

The Maple Leaf Lake is a manmade lake built in 1970. The community is open to its members and their visitors. To become a member, you may buy a residential property or building lot. The lake offers several amenities, including a community center, which you can rent for events, a pool, tennis courts, golf course, fishing piers, and several boat launches. Sewer and water are public. We have all underground electricity, put in brand new from the Knox county electrical plant, which is not far from the lake.

Elaan skimmed a couple more paragraphs, but it

wasn't anything interesting. Except the founder of the community named many of the streets after his children. It would be cool to have a street named after herself, she thought.

Josh tapped Elaan on the shoulder. "Open it," he said. Elaan was momentarily confused but then realized the brochure unfolded. Once open, the brochure showed a map. The large lake was in the center, and all around it were the streets of the community.

Josh grabbed one side of the map, and pointed to a spot in the upper right corner. "That's Crystal Circle," he said.

Elaan smiled. That was the address: 4801 Crystal Circle. Backtracking on the map, Crystal Circle seemed to be right off Jamaal Lane, which was connected to the main road that went all the way around the lake, Rasheeda's Way. She followed Rasheeda's Way on the map and saw that the visitor's center was just off Rasheeda's Way. "So we just follow this road," she said. "Take two turns and we're there?"

Josh nodded. "Yep," he said. "You ready?"

She thought about that for a second. Was she ready? Ready to see her mom? She was. It had been too long. "Yeah, let's go."

The roads in the Maple Leaf Community appeared to be deserted, too. Elaan wondered if this was normal for the lake community. The brochure gave the impression people bought second homes out here, rather than lived year round.

Following the map, they quickly found Crystal Circle, a cul de sac. To the right, they saw a small house numbered 4807. There was an empty lot next to that, and then another house further down. It was mainly hidden behind some trees, and they couldn't yet see the address on it, but Elaan suspected it was the house they needed, that it was 4801. Elaan could feel the tremor in her limbs as her nerves took hold. Was this it? Was this where they'd find her mother?

They slowed down as they approached the house. The landscape was strange. The cul de sac appeared to be a high point of the area, and the landscape around it descended downhill. The front of the house appeared to have a single story at ground level. But, you could see that the driveway sloped downward and that the basement was a walkout as you went down the hill.

When they got closer to the house, they saw lots of windows on the upper level, but they all had shades drawn. And they could hear noise coming from the house. They stopped the bike near the front yard and stared. Elaan got off the bike first. She looked at Josh, wondering if she could be imagining the strains of bass emanating from the building. But based on Josh's expression, she wasn't imagining things. He was hearing it, too.

He set the kickstand, and then she turned and walked toward the house, the sound getting louder. Dread coursed through her as they approached. Was this the wrong house? Had her mother left?

She trudged along the walkway to the house. Three steps led up to the front door. At the base of the steps, she could hear distinct phrases from the pumping music — counting. "One, two, three to the four."

She walked up the steps holding the black metal railing. The house had brown wood paneling, a light fixture next to the door, to turn on in the evenings. The thump of the music was louder. Would her mother really be jamming to dance music when the world was falling apart? No, she wouldn't, Elaan decided. This had to be the wrong house.

The numbers beneath the light read 4801. No, not the wrong house. Just the wrong people. Her mother had fled. Her mother wasn't here. She wanted to turn and leave. Josh tapped her on the shoulder. "You alright?" he asked softly.

"I don't think she's here," she said, feeling in her heart of hearts that they'd just journeyed all this way for nothing. They'd come to find her mother and her mother wasn't here.

"Well, someone's here," Josh said.

"I know. It's just," she started and stopped, not sure what she wanted to say. "It's just crazy that we've come all this way for nothing."

"We should still knock, see who's here," Josh said. "Maybe she left a note. Maybe she left something behind to help us find her."

Elaan hadn't thought of that. Of course. Her mother would know they might try to find her. She would leave a note, a clue, some type of message. But would these party people tell her? The singer accompanying the loud music said the word Tipsy, and she realized that she knew the song. It was a rapper, J-Kwon, and the song was called Tipsy. Sort of how she felt now. Like the world was tipsy turvy. Or maybe she meant topsy turvy. She sighed and nodded. "Alright, let's knock."

They took the remainder of the steps and knocked on the door. Nothing. No one answered. Elaan rapped her knuckles against the wood again, harder and louder this time. The music stopped, and she waited. A moment passed, then another. She heard rustling near the door. There was a peephole. She wondered if the person on the inside was staring at her.

The door opened, and a tall, gorgeous black man not wearing a shirt stood there. He was handsome, fit, dark skinned, luscious lips, bald head, sort of like a sleek African god. For some reason, the phrase, "Once you go black you never go back," flitted through her mind. She'd never seen someone so drop-dead gorgeous in real life and up close. She sputtered as she tried to remember what she'd wanted to say. Something about looking for her mother who'd given this as her last address. She'd planned to ask if he knew anything about the woman who'd lived here before him.

But before she could get any words out, the man turned his head, and yelled in a thick foreign accent, "Shonda, come out. It's your daughter."

<h1 style="text-align:center">23</h1>

The handsome man stepped aside, and a moment later, a woman came running toward the door. It took a moment for Elaan to realize it was her mother. Shonda, who normally wore a large afro or shoulder-length twists, had shaved her head so only an inch or so of hair remained. Her mother was wearing a sports bra, some type of flowy skirt, and no shoes.

The shirtless boytoy stepped aside with Shonda's arrival in the doorway, but he looked on with concern. He touched her mother's shoulder, an offer of comfort. Her mother seemed to ignore this, facing Elaan. Worry was etched on her face. "What's wrong? What happened?"

Elaan stared at her mother, at the hand on her shoulder, at the state of undress she was in, then she turned, brushed past Josh, and kept walking. She couldn't deal with this. Down the steps, up the slight slope of the ground, toward their bike. Away from the house. Away from that woman.

She got to the bike and stopped. She wanted to ride away, but she needed Josh. She turned back to the house and saw Josh was just a few feet from her.

"What are you doing?" he asked, his voice laced with worry.

"Lijah was right," she said. "We shouldn't have

come."

Josh shook his head. "You're not making any sense, Elaan," he said. He paused a moment, took a breath. "I know you didn't expect to find your mom with —" He trailed off.

Elaan followed his gaze to see her mother walking toward them, apparently having taken a moment to put on a pair of sandals. Josh left his sentence unfinished and stepped away as Shonda arrived.

"Sweetheart," she said, her voice sounding just the way it always had, yet different at the same time. It seemed like it had been a long time since she'd heard her mother speak to her that way: caring and concerned. "Are you alright?"

"Not as well as you," Elaan spat. "Partying and fucking some random stranger."

Shonda gritted her face and grabbed Elaan's arm, her voice low, but fierce. "I know you're upset about what you think is going on, but I am your mother, and you don't talk to me that way. Do you understand?"

Elaan stared at her mother, the fury still bubbling inside her. "My mother is dead," she said, yanking her arm loose from her mother's grip.

She turned, side-stepping the bike, and began to walk away. She had no idea where she'd go in this crazy world she didn't understand, but she knew she didn't want to be here.

She heard footsteps behind her. "Elaan, your father was only supposed to tell you about me, about this place, in a dire emergency. Is he..." she started, but the rest of the words seemed choked in her throat. "Is your father dead?"

Like her mother gave a damn. She had Mr. Tall,

Dark, and Handsome at her beck and call. Elaan kept walking and didn't bother to answer. But her mother didn't let it go. Shonda jogged and caught up. Now she was walking beside Elaan. "Is this really how you want to behave? You came a thousand miles just to walk away?"

Elaan kept walking, but her steps didn't have the same fervor. Her mother had a point. They had come all this way. But they'd come all this way to see someone who was in hiding, not someone partying it up with some sexy-as-hell dude.

"Where is Lijah?" her mother asked.

Elaan stopped walking. Guilt careened through her. Lijah had come with her. Lijah was supposed to be here, too. Only, he'd stayed on a train with a psycho underground conductor, for the sole purpose of keeping her safe. She turned to her mother, and she felt nothing but disgust. Her father missed this woman. Her father, even though he knew she wasn't dead, was grieving the loss of her presence. Her father was feeling guilty that he might have condemned this woman to death.

Yet, what was the great Shonda Woodson doing? Partying with a man half her age in her secret love nest.

"So, you've just been here partying this whole time? Did you even think about us, miss us for even a second?"

Shonda's face tightened, and she blew out a long, steadying breath. In a soft tone, she said, "I have not been here partying." She shook her head and glanced back at the house, which Elaan had managed to trek a full block from in her anger. Her mother turned back to her. "Amadu got the speakers fixed today, and he wanted to test them out. Today was an unusual day."

Amadu. What a name. Elaan sighed and spotted the house in the distance. The front door was closed, and Josh was standing near their bike. She'd abandoned him all because she was mad. She hated that her mother was right. She was acting childish.

But right now she didn't care. Maybe it was immature, but she was seventeen and she was tired of being mature. She was tired of having to be an adult while everyone around her crumbled. First her father, back in the compound, and now her mother, living like a hippy teen on a commune with some guy young enough to be her son. "So, Amadu's your boyfriend?"

Shonda shook her head. "I am married," she said firmly. "To your father, and I have never once been unfaithful to him. Amadu is an immune. I offered to let him stay with me, and he's been helping me. He knows things about survival that I just didn't. He's trapped animals for us to eat, knows an amazing amount about which plants are edible, and was able to fix the broken stereo so we could dance, because dancing is better than crying over the fact that your children are out there, and one of them thinks you're dead. Because dancing is better than worrying that you're going to go out and make people sick. OK?"

Elaan stared at her mother, her anger slowly waning. She didn't have a whole lot of fight left in her as she looked at her mother, who she now really looked at. Yes, the hair was a big difference, the most noticeable one, the one that immediately found you. But everything about her mother was different. She was much thinner than before. She'd lost weight, either through not having enough food, or through an anxiety-suppressed appetite. She also had more wrinkles on her face. Her eyes, a beautiful chestnut brown that always seemed to sparkle, seemed completely lackluster, as if they'd been drained of everything that made them special. Shonda looked like being here had aged her ten years.

"Please come back to the house," Shonda said. "I want to know why you're here. I want to meet your friend." She gave her daughter a hopeful glance.

Elaan nodded and her mother smiled at her, a broad grin that made her look more like her old self: happy, peaceful. Or maybe that was the way her mother made her feel — happy and peaceful. At least, she thought that was it. Or had she been misremembering it? Had the feelings of loss clouded all her memories of her mother? Were they still shrouded in the veil of wanting, the veil she had worn the last three months, that of wanting nothing more than to talk to her mother again?

Shonda waited for Elaan to start moving, then walked beside her. Shonda smiled and spoke softly. "I'm really glad you're here," she said.

Elaan didn't respond. She wasn't sure she was glad to be here. It wasn't what she had expected, and though her mother's explanation for Amadu made sense, she still sensed there was something off about the situation, something her mother wasn't sharing with her.

They walked in silence until they reached Josh, who stepped back as they arrived. Elaan eyed him curiously for a moment, then realized it was her mother who was causing his reaction. Her mother wasn't supposed to be contagious with everyday contact, but given that Josh was one step away from being a carrier himself, she could see why he'd given them a wide berth.

"Mom," Elaan said. "This is Josh Wells."

Shonda narrowed her eyes at Josh and took a step back from him now. "Are you Kingston's son?"

Josh nodded but didn't speak.

"You got the trial vaccine, the same one Lijah got?"

Josh nodded again, and Shonda pursed her lips. Elaan was surprised at how much her mother knew.

"Let's go inside so we can talk more freely," Shonda said, looking around at the deserted street, as if she expected someone to come along. Shonda turned down the driveway toward the house. "The garage is this way. You should park your bike inside so no one comes along and takes it."

Elaan grabbed hold of the bike's handlebars and guided it down the driveway following her mother. Josh walked along the other side of the bike. "We're staying?" he asked. Elaan nodded.

His lips parted as if he intended to say something more, but he apparently thought better of it and closed his mouth. They followed several paces behind her mother as she headed down the driveway and opened the garage. Elaan's mouth popped open. There was a car. A little blue Prius.

On the other side of the garage, at least a dozen plastic storage boxes were stacked, lining the wall. Elaan looked at her mother curiously. Shonda said nothing, simply motioning them to bring the bike inside. They wheeled it in and Shonda closed the garage door after them. The room was dark at first, but then a light came on. Her mother had electricity, too. Like Lee. Though, she should have known that from the party music they were playing.

Her mother went to the center of the garage door and did something, but Elaan couldn't see what. "Locking it," her mother said. "Amadu must have seen us coming back and unlocked it for us. We don't want anyone trying to take stuff."

"The car has gas?" Elaan asked.

"Yeah," Shonda replied. "It's got a full tank and a battery maintainer. I knew the car might have to sit a while, so I got one before things got too crazy. Normally, if a car sits for too long, the battery will eventually drain and die. The maintainer keeps it going. If you're handy, you can disconnect the battery, or disconnect things like the clock. Amadu and I keep talking about taking it out for a spin, but we're both a little hesitant about being robbed or followed back here and have someone break in."

Shonda looked at her daughter and Josh, then said, "Come on, we should go upstairs." Shonda walked past the boxes and the car to a door in the rear of the garage. She opened it and it led to a stairway. This made Elaan consider the house's layout, and she realized that due to the slope of the ground, which seemed to continue downhill, the garage was beneath the living area of the house. She walked over to the door, which her mother was holding open. Josh followed behind Elaan, though he looked hesitant. Perhaps he even regretted coming.

At the top of the stairs they entered a room with high ceilings and polished wood floors. To the left was a room with sofas, an easy chair, a fireplace, a bookshelf, and a shelf with a stereo and television. To the right, the floor was tile, clearly a kitchen area. A refrigerator, stove, marble countertops, maple cabinets, and in the center of the room a small circular table flanked by two folding chairs. There was more to the house. A hallway jutted off the main room, and Elaan assumed the bedrooms and bathrooms were down the corridor.

Elaan and Josh walked toward the fireplace. Shonda came up after them, smiling broadly. It was so different, so weird to see this smile she hadn't seen in so long.

Shonda walked over to the easy chair and sat, motioning hem to sit on the nearby sofa. "So, tell me everything," her mother said.

24

Elaan was perched on the end of the sofa closest to her mother. Josh joined her, but edged as far from Shonda as possible without appearing rude.

"Tell us, first," Elaan said, as she eyed her mother, then peered toward the hallway to make sure Amadu wasn't nearby. "Why are you living here with this guy?"

Shonda's smile faded, but she still seemed upbeat. "I don't know how much you know about the circumstances in which I left," she started.

"Nothing," Elaan said in a clipped voice. "Dad told me that you were dead. I believed him. It never occurred to me that anyone would lie to their child about that. I just assumed we didn't have a funeral because the disease was so contagious. So, I grieved and mourned for you for the last three months. I felt awful because I didn't even get to say goodbye. I missed you every day for the last three months. And then, a few days ago, Lijah told me you were alive, and that you were a carrier. That you could make people sick."

Shonda sat up straighter, and looked her daughter in the eye. She reached out and touched her hand. "I'm sorry it was so hard for you," she said softly. "I really.... I just... I'm sorry. I didn't want you to hurt like that, baby. I just wanted you to be safe."

Elaan slid her hand away from her mother's. "It doesn't matter now," she said. "Just tell me what you wanted to tell me, about the — y'know, 'circumstances' in which you left."

Shonda stared intently at her daughter and looked briefly as if she intended to hug Elaan or offer some other comfort or apology. But then Shonda took a deep breath and shook her head. "OK," she said. "There will be time for apologies later. You want to know how I left. Your father learned I'm related to Mark Dayton, so, on the off chance that I might also be a carrier, too, he tested my blood and learned I was. Only, I'm a bit different from my brother. I'm a carrier of the less contagious strand, Helnoan-A.

"People tend to get it when they come in contact with bodily fluids — a lot of them. You only get that level of fluid when you're taking care of the sick, when they're vomiting or bleeding constantly, and it's almost impossible to stay completely clear. For most people, I'm not going to make them sick." She turned to Josh. "I understand your concern, and I want you to know it's incredibly unlikely that exposure to me will turn you into a carrier. I'll try to stay at a comfortable distance."

Elaan asked the question that had been noodling around in her brain ever since her mother first spoke to Josh. "How do you know about Josh? You've been in hiding the entire time we were in the compound."

Shonda turned to her daughter. "Until the internet went down for me last month, I was communicating with your father using email."

"Isn't that dangerous?" Elaan asked.

Shonda shook her head. "We didn't send each

other emails," she said. "Before I went into hiding, he created an email account we both knew the username and password for. To talk to him, I'd create a draft message, but not send it. Later, he would log in and respond to the draft. We never actually sent the email. We just had lots of draft messages. He told me things about you, about Lijah, about his guilt over what had happened, how he wished he could do things differently."

Elaan swallowed, not sure she wanted to think about her father wallowing in self-pity. What a shame her mother couldn't have convinced him to buck up and get his act together. She looked at her mother and motioned her to continue.

"So, I was able to communicate with him until a little over a month ago. And your father knew about Amadu. He understands. He knows it's hard out here."

Elaan raised an eyebrow. Was she serious? "You told him you were living with a guy half your age in the middle of nowhere?"

Her mother gave her a hard look. "I told him that Amadu moved in, and he thought it was safer for me not to be alone. He knows there's nothing going on between us."

Elaan sighed, still not happy with that last tidbit. Maybe Amadu was the reason her dad couldn't get his act together. He was probably depressed that the wife he'd risked everything to save was shacking up with some young stud. The anger that had surged inside her when Amadu had opened the door returned. "And who is Amadu exactly?"

"He's a grad student at the University of Illinois. He's originally from Ghana, but he's been here since he was eighteen. He's majoring in chemical engineering, and when the campus closed in May, he didn't have anywhere to go. He was supposed to do a summer internship with one of the professors in the lab, but it got canceled because of all the sickness. The university shut down for the summer. If things were normal, they'd be open now, but I don't know if the campuses can reopen with so many people gone."

"Mom," Elaan cut in, not caring whether the university was open or not. "How did you meet him? And what are you two?"

"We're not a couple, Elaan," she said. "I've told you that. He's a friend, someone who's been helping."

"But he's living with you, and you've known him for, what, a month?"

"Amadu was alone out here, like me. When the semester ended in May, his professor, the one he was supposed to intern with, invited him out here for the summer. The professor owns a house on the other side of the lake, on Kendall Drive." Shonda pointed to the row of windows along the back of the house. Elaan looked out, but all she saw was trees.

"Well," Shonda said. "About three weeks after Amadu got here, the professor and all his family were dead. They'd somehow contracted the virus. That's when Amadu realized he was immune. He'd been too close to them to not have caught the virus. Since he was alone in the professor's house, he had to decide what to do. He buried the bodies, and stayed in the house.

"While the family had planned to buy more supplies once they arrived, they didn't have a chance. There weren't many supplies. The fact that they'd been too sick to eat was the reason Amadu had the amount of food he did. He took the cash the professor had and went to town to buy supplies. But he knew it wasn't enough. To make his supplies last as long as he could, Amadu decided to fish and trap. That's when I saw him for the first time.

"I'd driven out on one of my last supply runs. I'd been stockpiling things, and could tell I'd need to hunker down soon. People were becoming scary, dangerous, and very primal, with everyone you met looking at you as if the key to their survival was dispatching you and taking your things.

"I drove the long way around to the house, figuring I might not get out that much afterwards, when I saw Amadu on the dock. He was barefoot, and wearing overalls and a straw hat. I could see enough of him to know he was young, and he reminded me a little bit of Lijah, so I pulled over and asked if he was alright. He was surprised, but he told me he was fine and that he lived around the bend. He told me the house number, and I made a mental note of it. A few days later, I decided to walk over.

"There wasn't much else to do here. There's a TV, but it doesn't get any stations anymore. When I knocked on his door, he was there, and he was fairly bored, too. It's easy to go stir crazy when you're alone so much. Anyway, Amadu and I talked, and he told me he was immune. I didn't quite trust him yet, but I did think he was a nice young man. I went over a couple more times and then, one day, I asked if he wanted to come with me to get gas. He agreed and we drove up Route 150 until we hit town. We stopped at Casey's, bought gas for the car, and filled a couple of five-gallon gasoline drums, in case we needed gasoline later and the stations were closed. I had taken him to his place, just to drop him off, and he invited me in for a minute. We left the car parked in the driveway, which you could see from the house. After we were inside, I happened to look out and see men trying to steal the car. They had a slim jim and were trying to get the door open. There was a pickup truck parked on the street, and we think maybe they followed us from the gas station. Amadu grabbed his shotgun and managed to scare them off with a warning shot. That made me realize just how vulnerable I was being out here alone. I asked Amadu if he wanted to move in here with me. There would be two of us, and, the people who'd followed us didn't know about this house. They only knew about Amadu's. He agreed, and we've been living here together ever since. And truthfully, I got the better deal. He's taught me way more than I ever knew about survival."

Elaan sighed and looked around the house. It felt big, and it would probably be scary living here alone. Especially after guys tried to steal her car. She was softening a bit toward her mother, after hearing the story. Maybe shacking up with the stud wasn't so unreasonable after all. "Where is he?"

"I think he's trying to give us some privacy, and let us catch up. I believe he's in his room."

Elaan looked down the hallway. She didn't see him emerge.

"So," her mother said, getting Elaan's attention. "Why did you guys leave the safety of the scientist protection unit?"

"Because it wasn't safe anymore," Elaan said, grimacing at the memory. "They'd found out about Josh and Lijah and wanted them at Facility One."

Her mother's eyes widened and she leaned

forward. "How did they find out?"

Elaan shook her head. "I don't know. We just knew that they had. One of the generals received orders to take Lijah and Josh there. And he was supposed to take me somewhere, too. Somewhere in Virginia where they experiment on immunes. We only found out because the general's wife gave us a heads-up. If we hadn't left, they would've taken us the next day."

Shonda bit her lip, took a deep breath, and then steadied herself as she looked at Elaan, then Josh, then back to her daughter. "If the three of you left together, where is Lijah?"

25

Elaan stared at her mother, her stomach clenching as her thoughts turned to her brother standing in the boxcar holding a gun to Willie. Lijah had told her to run, to save herself, and now he was…? God, where was he?

She closed her eyes, unable to look at her mother. A hand began rubbing her back gently and she heard Josh's voice as he scooted closer to her. He spoke softly but clearly as he explained how they'd left the complex, how Lijah had thought it was a good idea to catch the train, their run-in with Willie, how Elaan had paid with her mother's ring rather than kowtowing to Willie's demands for "companionship." And then, Josh told of their departure from the train, how Lijah had stayed behind to make sure that Willie didn't alert authorities.

When Josh finished, there was silence. An unsettling silence that made Elaan fear the sound that might break it. Would it be anger? Anger at Elaan for forcing Lijah to make such a choice? Anger at Willie, the government, the situation? Or just grief? Lijah was gone, and they knew nothing more. If Willie had somehow regained the upper hand, what would he have done with Lijah? Probably shot him and dumped him off the train. Her brother's corpse could be rotting near the tracks somewhere, being picked

182

apart by the vultures or eaten by God knew what, like those people they'd taken the bike from. If he were dead, killed by Willie, they'd never really know Lijah's fate. And something about that thought made Elaan feel as if she were drowning. As if all the air were being sucked from her lungs.

She didn't want Lijah to be dead. Not because he'd wanted to protect her. She was crying now. She could feel the tears sliding down her cheeks, and she closed her eyes and wiped away the tears.

"Elaan," she heard her mother say, as the hand on her back slid away. She opened her eyes in time to see her mother crouching before her. From the corner of her eye, she saw Josh had moved to the opposite side of the sofa, his eyes fixed on her mother.

She looked down at the brown face in front of her. Same kind brown eyes that had always greeted her in her times of need. "Baby," her mother said. "It's alright. Lijah's going to be alright. Don't cry."

Elaan shook her head. "Mom," she said, her voice breaking. "You don't know that. You don't know what happened to Lijah. And if it's anything bad, it'll be my fault."

Her mother set a hand on Elaan's shoulder and stroked gently. "No, it will only be the fault of that awful man on the train. He's the only one to blame. Or if you don't want to blame him, blame me. Blame me and your father. Blame us for teaching Lijah that he should protect his baby sister. He did what was right, Elaan. He did what was important, and I know your brother. He's fine. I can feel it, right here."

Shonda touched her chest. Her mother could feel that Lijah wasn't dead. It seemed stupid, yet Elaan was heartened by it. She stared at her mother, at that twinkle in her eyes, at the line of her nose, at the set of her lips, firm and reassuring, and could tell her mother meant what she said. She really believed Lijah was fine. Her mother's confidence had the effect it often did on Elaan. It made her feel better. It made her feel that maybe her mother was right. That Lijah had managed Willie somehow, that everything would be OK. Only, if that was true....

"But he isn't here," Elaan pointed out. "Wouldn't he be here if he were alright?"

The corners of her mother's mouth turned downward, as if she'd intended to frown, but managed to stop herself. Shonda turned her head and looked toward the window, then back at Elaan. "There are a lot of reasonable explanations for why he's not here that don't involve him being dead," her mother said. "The first one being that you two had a bike. That had to make your trip quicker."

Despite its obviousness, Elaan hadn't thought of that. Her mother was right. The bike had cut their travel time by several days.

"Also, he may have chosen not to come," she said. "Josh was pretty nice about how he said it, but he indicated that Lijah only promised to get you here. That he really wouldn't come here except to bring you. Perhaps he just figured Josh would get you here, so he didn't need to bother. He was angry with me."

Elaan watched her mother for any clues about what had happened between her and Lijah. Yes, he knew she was a carrier, and he'd taken the vaccine because he thought she'd died, but his anger toward her seemed so much more personal than that. Shonda furrowed her brow, her teeth nipping her bottom lip. The anguish in her eyes indicated her mother was deeply troubled by Lijah's feelings toward her.

"Why was he mad at you, Mom?" Elaan, asked, her tone even, but still firm enough to convey she expected a response.

Her mother snapped out of her moment of self-pity and looked at her daughter with fresher eyes. She opened her mouth to speak but then turned to look at Josh. "It's not important," she said.

"Yes it is," Elaan countered. "I mean, what would cause him to be so angry that he'd let us think he'd died, rather than come here and tell us he was OK?"

Her mother looked at Josh again. "Maybe he's just worried I'll make him a carrier, like me. It's very unlikely, but look at your friend. He's still hesitant. Lijah might not want to come at all."

"But that's not what you said, Mom," she interrupted again. "You said he was angry with you. Why?"

Her mother's eyes darted to Josh and then back at Elaan. She paused a moment and said, "Because he blames me for not telling him that I was alive, for him not knowing that he was in quarantine more for show than anything else. The last time we talked, it wasn't good. He was so angry at me. And rightly so. I should've trusted you. Both of you. And even though I knew I had caused this for Lijah, it didn't occur to me that my lie would hurt you, too. Because you were immune, I thought you were going to be fine. Yet, they only know you're immune because your father had you tested. He had you tested because of me, and now they want to hurt you because you're immune. All roads lead back to me and my lies."

Shonda rubbed her forehead and sighed. Elaan had never really seen her mother like this. Yes, she'd made mistakes before, but she'd always had this attitude of, "I messed up. I'm sorry. Let's move on. Let's fix it." Now, she didn't look like she wanted to move on. She looked like she was defeated by her mistakes, like she didn't have the energy to fix it.

Elaan, at least part of her, wanted to put a hand on her mother's shoulder and tell her it would be alright, that things weren't as bad as they seemed. Yet, none of that was true. Things were bad. Lijah was missing, and her mother's lies had cost them all so much.

Her mother stood back up, took a deep breath, and then smiled at Elaan. "You know what," she said. "Don't worry about me or Lijah. I'm just really glad you're here."

Elaan nodded, realizing that even though there was anger simmering at the surface, she was glad, too. Everything else aside, she had missed her mother. A month ago. Hell, a week ago, she would have paid any price to have her mother sitting this close to her, alive and healthy. She had her wish, and now she wasn't even appreciating it. "I'm glad I'm here, too, Mom."

Shonda reached out and hugged Elaan, the embrace feeling familiar and warm. It was like being home again. She settled in, enjoying the feel of her mother's arms, even though they were thinner than they had been before. And despite everything else, her mother still seemed to smell the same: rough, yet mellow with a hint of sweetness.

They stayed in their embrace another moment, then released each other.

"You guys are probably tired and hungry," Shonda said, standing up. "There's some food I can get you, or you can take a nap. There are three bedrooms, so Elaan, it probably makes the most sense for us to double up in the biggest room. Josh, you can have the third bedroom. It's got bunk beds. When Lijah comes, you two can share."

"Thanks, Mrs. Woodson," Josh said.

Shonda smiled at them both. "Hungry? I can make you something?"

"Mom," Elaan said. "I'm not that tired, and Josh and I ate already. I thought maybe we could just sit for a minute."

"Sure," Shonda said, sitting back down. "Sure."

26

Elaan and Josh had scooted together on the sofa, though they didn't say much. Shonda had sat with them for a few minutes, but then insisted they eat. She'd gone to the kitchen and was futzing around. She'd explained that they were fortunate to still have electricity. They were on the same power grid as a nearby military institution, as well as a prison. The government had worked hard to ensure that the base and prison had electricity.

"Though, there was a rumor that they starved all the prisoners to death," her mother said in a hushed tone as she poured water into a pot. "I heard that more than a month ago. I haven't been out since then to find out more. Not to mention, people aren't the chattiest with strangers. Everyone's just really weary of the virus."

Shonda sat down. "The lentils are in the water cooking. I boil the water first. There's no way to know if the water treatment plant is working properly. There's no indication the water's bad, but I still boil it first, just in case. There's drinking water in a glass flask in the refrigerator. It's been boiled and cooled."

Elaan nodded. "So what happened a month ago?" she asked. "Lee, the guy we stayed with last night, alluded to it. There seems to have been a shift then. A shift from people to nobody."

Shonda knitted her brow. "I know what he's talking about. It was clear and obvious that there was a change, but I don't know what happened. I don't know what caused it. I only know that we lost our internet last month. Before that, I could communicate with your father. He'd tell me how you were, how Lijah was, send me his data. I could read news stories on the sites that were still around. There was the Martial Law, there was increasing sickness. Increasing death. Everything was bad news. And then one day, we couldn't log on. Things just seemed to cease."

"And you don't know why?"

Her mother shook her head. "No," she admitted. "At first I just took it at face value. I thought the service provider we were using had maintenance problems, but no one to fix them. I figured it was just a simple problem related to our company. But then, when we went out, there were fewer and fewer people. Everything seemed to change. I don't know what happened. I don't know why that was, but it seemed weird. And now, you come here and tell me that the compound stopped getting food deliveries a month ago. The man you stayed with said there was a change, too. I wish I knew what it was. I wish I knew what happened."

Shonda's eyes had a far-off look, like she was thinking. She'd bitten her lip and was deep in concentration on some idea, Elaan could tell. It always seemed best to let her be, when she was like that. Elaan was silent for a moment, but curiosity got the better of her. "So do you have a theory?"

Her mother shrugged. "Nothing particularly feasible."

Elaan nodded, and Josh went to the restroom.

Once he was out of earshot, Shonda leaned in and said, "So, your father mentioned Josh in his earlier emails. He said that Lijah and Josh were friends. I didn't know that you knew him well."

Elaan wondered about Lijah's feelings for Josh. About how her father had perceived their relationship. She wasn't sure what her mother was getting at. "Josh was Lijah's friend first, but he and I have become friends, too."

Her mother nodded, though she seemed to be scrutinizing everything about Elaan's expression. "He was an OK person to travel with? He didn't do anything to make you uncomfortable, did he?"

Elaan felt herself blush. "Mom, Josh didn't do anything to me, OK? He's really nice, but I don't want to talk about me and Josh, alright?"

Her mother took in a short breath and narrowed her eyes. "You *and* Josh? You and he are together?"

They heard the toilet flush, so Elaan looked down the hallway. Saved by the flush. She wasn't going to answer her mother's question, and she knew her mother wouldn't press her on it with Josh around. A moment later, Josh was seated next to Elaan, fairly close, and Shonda watched them with new interest.

Shonda struck up a conversation with Josh, managing to talk about subjects that weren't touchy, yet still being engaging and friendly. It was an art she'd developed being a college professor. When she was younger, Elaan had thought all parents were chatty and conversant with friends who came over. But, as she grew older, she learned it wasn't the case. Or perhaps Shonda had a way of making her friends enjoy the conversation, rather than feeling put upon or obligated.

"I was so sorry to hear about your mother's passing," Shonda said. "I only met her a couple of times, but she was a really great lady."

Josh nodded, and muttered thanks, but Elaan was intrigued. She had no idea her mother knew Josh's mother. She hadn't really thought about it before, but she suddenly wanted to know everything.

"I didn't know you knew her," Elaan said.

Her mother smiled, nodded. "Yes, Jane and I met when your father started the project. You know, he and Kingston were on the original Helnoan task force, prior to it being airborne. So, we all had dinner, at Zaika in Arlington. It was me and your father and Kingston and Jane. She and I swapped numbers so we'd have somebody to talk to about how much our husbands worked. Well, ostensibly, that's what we exchanged numbers for, but we didn't really end up chatting much. We both were busy enough in our own lives that we didn't have time to commiserate. And then, in the end, the way she died... " Shonda shook her head at the memory, as if it was horrifying.

Elaan looked at her mother curiously. Then she turned to Josh, who seemed to be staring at her mother, too. "Yes, the virus is an awful way to die," Elaan said tentatively.

Shonda looked at Elaan, then at Josh. Her mother and Josh appeared to have some secret communication going on. Their eyes were saying something to each other and Elaan wasn't privy to it. "What's going on?" Elaan asked.

Josh eyed Shonda with a modicum of distrust and asked, "Do you know?"

"About how she got the virus?" Shonda asked.

Josh grimaced, then nodded.

Shonda nodded in response.

Elaan looked at her mother, then Josh. His face paled and he frowned. He was clearly unhappy, and Elaan didn't want to make him more upset, but she also wanted answers. She turned to her mother. "How did Josh's mother get the virus?"

Shonda watched Josh, assessing his demeanor, and then turned to her daughter. "You know, it's not important how his mother died," she said softly. "I shouldn't have brought it up. It wasn't my place."

Elaan stared at her mother, irritated. "You know and Josh knows. Still you think it's so unimportant for me to know. Is lying to me the only thing you're able to do?"

Shonda shook her head emphatically. "I'm not trying to lie to you or hide the truth," she said, leaning forward, apology in her tone. "It's not that I don't want you to know. It's just that I thought, if Josh isn't comfortable talking about it, we wouldn't discuss it right now."

"Well, you didn't even give him a chance," Elaan said. "You're not in control of the world. You don't get to dole out the bits of knowledge you want people to have and keep all the secrets."

"Elaan," Josh said, softly. She turned to him and instantly regretted what she'd just said.

He looked her in the eye and said, "I don't want to talk about my mother's death. It's not a good subject for me, but I'll tell you the reason, and then let's not talk about it, OK?"

Elaan nodded, feeling a stab of guilt. She'd gotten so caught up in anger at her mother that she hadn't considered Josh's feelings. He really didn't seem like he wanted to talk about it. "You know," she said, taking his hand. "We can talk about it later. I don't have to know now."

He shook his head. "It's fine. We've already started. Might as well finish."

"Alright, but just if you want to."

He nodded. "I told you that my mom was a spy. Well, she was in charge of several high-level intelligence programs. She was infected intentionally by someone who wanted to shut down her department. It was a fairly high-level investigation, because the way she was infected was also used to infect most of her staff and several of their families. It's why my father wanted me vaccinated. He wasn't sure if I might still be a target, even after her death. After my mom died, I got thrown into quarantine. My dad got me and Lijah out a few days later, but that's the reason I took the vaccine. Yes, my father didn't want me to be a danger in the world, but he also didn't want the world to come after me, the way it had my mother."

27

The mood was somber after Josh's admission. While glad to know, Elaan felt a little stung that Josh hadn't told her this before. Though, maybe she was being whiny. She hadn't really asked him about his mother's death. It was something she thought she'd understood, and she'd specifically avoided it after learning her own mother was alive.

Still, it was bizarre to learn that Josh's mother the spy had actually died as a direct result of her spying activities, not chance. Clearly wanting to change the mood, Shonda offered to show them their rooms. Josh took the room across the hall from the bathroom, a small bedroom with bunk beds and a window facing the front of the house. The curtains were drawn, but Elaan walked over and peeked out front. Quiet and still.

"Do people live around here?" she asked her mother.

Shonda shook her head. "I think this area was primarily summer people. I'm surprised more people didn't come out here to get away from the virus in the city. But it's been pretty deserted. A little further down, I think there are more people."

Elaan nodded, and her mother beckoned her over. "Let's let Josh get settled while I show you our room."

Elaan offered a smile and a nod to Josh as she left and followed her mother to the end of the hall. The room was twice the size of Josh's and filled with natural light. Windows ran the length of the side and rear walls. The shades were open and Elaan could see thick trees behind the house. She turned to her mother. "So, where is the lake?"

"Bottom of the hill, through the trees," she said. "There's a path to it. I imagine you can see it once the leaves fall off the trees. Mark apparently designed the house himself. He was into architecture."

Elaan bit her lip. "This was Dayton's house?"

Shonda nodded. "Yeah," she said. "I didn't get to know him because of the virus and him being killed, but I tried to read what I could find. I rummaged through some of the personal belongings here."

Elaan looked around the room, wondering what it was like when the preacher who'd caused such havoc on the world had lived here. She wondered what had caused him to build himself a nice house in the woods. She wondered if he was an unscrupulous pastor who'd stolen from his church to fund this house.

"How did you end up here?"

Shonda fidgeted with a window shade, then sighed. "Your father took charge of liquidating Dayton's estate. He sold it to me — new me — Jenny S. Rhodes. I have deeds, paperwork, a fake passport, driver's license, but nobody cares. Nobody cares who you are, just whether or not you're sick."

Her mother blew out, then forced a smile. She held out a hand to Elaan. "How about I take your bag?"

Elaan shook her head and looked down at the

backpack in her hand. She didn't want to part with it, or have it unpacked by anyone else.

"If your fake name is Jenny, why does your roommate call you Shonda? Why does he know about us?"

Shonda sat down on the bed and bade Elaan to join her. Elaan declined, leaning against the wall. "Well," her mother said. "I'd initially told him my name was Jenny, but half the times he called me Jenny, I didn't answer, so I told him most people called me my middle name, Shonda."

"Why have a fake name if you weren't going to use it?"

Her mother eyed her pointedly. "This world is not the one you remember, baby. It's lonely and sometimes a bit of truth in the loneliness helps," she said. "Plus, it didn't seem that detrimental. It was only Amadu, and he still thinks my given name was Jenny. All the records that are left say that Shonda Woodson is dead, so a Jenny Shonda Rhodes matters a lot less. At least not when I'm holed up in a house in the woods, simply trying to survive."

On some level it made sense. On another level it seemed reckless. But given the number of people they'd met, how likely was it that someone was alive and around who could connect Jenny Shonda Rhodes with Shonda Yvette Woodson? And, Elaan wondered briefly, if she had stayed with Lee for long enough, would she have eventually trusted him and told him her name? Perhaps. It was hard to lie to someone every single day when it was just the two of you, when the rest of the world was so far away.

She sighed as she stared at her mother, who sat on the bed. Elaan didn't have anything else to say, but her mother watched her expectantly. Only, Elaan liked the silence. She liked the things not said, for some reason. Perhaps Lijah was right about the truth. It wasn't that great, and it wasn't necessary. This new Shonda, was her mother in looks, but she wasn't quite her mother in spirit. She was a hybrid animal, one who felt the need to share some nugget of truth with the man she lived with, yet she had happily abandoned Elaan for this new life, not caring if Elaan knew. And she'd just moments ago been willing to keep the truth about Josh's mother from her. Only, Amadu had known who Elaan was the moment he'd seen her, so her mother hadn't forgotten about her. She'd told him about her, must even have had a picture to show him.

Everything about her mother was different and confusing. She walked over and sat next to her mother on the bed. Without a word, she wrapped her arms around her and held her, and suddenly this woman felt like Mom again. And the arms were warm, with a beating heart touched to another, and her mother stroked her hair. This was the only thing that was right in this crazy, messed-up world. She pulled free from her mother. "You know," she said. "I actually am tired. I think I'm going to take a nap."

Shonda smiled, and said, "Good idea. It's been a long day."

Her mother headed to the door. Elaan put the backpack aside in the corner, then remembered the flash drive. "Mom," she called. "Wait." Her mother turned and walked back toward her.

Elaan rummaged around in the backpack until she found the flash drive, and pulled it out. "Dad put this in my bag, but I don't know why."

Shonda walked over. "We have a computer," she said. "No internet, but it should read that. You want to take a look?"

Elaan nodded. She followed her mother back to the main room. In the corner next to the fireplace, was a square table with a laptop. Shonda opened it and turned it on. The computer took a minute to warm up.

Josh came out of his bedroom and walked over to them. "What's going on?"

"Mom's going to check out the USB drive," Elaan said, watching over her mother's shoulder as the laptop finally booted and her mother stuck the drive in the slot. Josh nodded and stood next to Elaan as the drive appeared on the desktop and Shonda clicked to open it.

There was a single file folder on the drive. Shonda double-clicked and a little window appeared on the screen with the words, "Enter password."

Shonda looked up at Elaan. "You know what it is?"

Elaan shook her head. "No idea."

"Is there something you guys always use as a password," Josh asked.

Elaan shrugged The Netflix password was the only one that they all used and knew. "Umm, splish4splash?"

Shonda laughed. "If that's it, then he probably didn't want to protect it that much." She typed it in and a moment later the folder opened. "Okkkkkaaaay," she said. "Didn't expect that."

Inside the folder were several other folders and a single text file called Sweppy. "What's Sweppy?" Josh asked.

Elaan gritted her teeth, hoping her mother wouldn't answer. It was embarrassing enough that her parents had pet names for each other, let alone that they named files using them.

"It's short for sweet pea," Shonda said, clicking the file open.

A fairly short note appeared.

S.

I have enclosed all the data from the vaccine trials along with immune data. It has information I think will be helpful. Some data you haven't seen from K.

-J.

Elaan stared at the screen, then tapped her mother on the shoulder. "Who is K?"

Shonda looked briefly at her daughter, then back at the screen. "Kingston."

Her mother's voice had been calm when she spoke, but Elaan thought there was an edge to it, something peculiar. She wondered if her mother was lying to her. Again. Elaan sighed and walked away, not wanting to confront her mother. Not in front of Josh, whose own mother was, in fact, dead. She had been given something Josh hadn't — a miraculous return from the dead of someone she loved. She couldn't fight with her mom in front of him. Company manners had to be in full play while he was around. Josh had been her rock while they were traveling, but she wished he were gone so she could talk candidly with her mother.

Shonda had clicked open a file and leaned in closer, scrutinizing the data. "Do you see any patterns?" Elaan asked.

"Not yet." Her mother must have really missed her, because she'd managed to avoid all sarcasm in that reply. Of course she hadn't found any patterns. She'd just opened the file. Elaan hated waiting, though. Patience wasn't her strong suit.

Her mother turned and looked at her. "Y'know, sweetheart, there are a lot of files here and it's going to take me a while to go through them. Why don't you two get settled, have a nap, or grab a book to read." She pointed to the far wall, which had a floor to ceiling bookshelf. Elaan wasn't sure what kind of books would be there, or even if she was in the mood to read. "I'll let you know the minute I find anything interesting."

"OK, Mom," she said simply, and walked away. Instead of heading for the bookshelf, she walked over to the kitchen. The dull hum of the refrigerator's motor sharpened as she got closer. She opened up the fridge, and a strong, pungent odor wafted out. Some vacuum-sealed milk packages were on the top shelf, but immediately beneath them was a plate of fish. Whole fish, heads and everything, stared back at her. Probably her mother, or more likely Amadu, had caught them. Wrinkling her nose, Elaan closed the refrigerator door and turned to find Josh behind her.

"Hey," he said. "I think I accidentally put some of your things in my bag. You wanna come get them?"

Elaan raised an eyebrow, wondering what exactly of hers could've gotten into Josh's bag. She could think of nothing, but followed him to his room.

Josh closed the door and spoke softly. "What's

going on?"

Elaan had no idea what he was talking about. "What do you mean?"

"What data did my dad have that the two of them couldn't figure out on their own?"

Elaan shook her head, confused, and whispered back. "I don't know. I'm as confused as you are."

He frowned. "Do you think your mother is telling the truth? That she really has no idea what the link might be?"

Well, so much for not airing dirty laundry in front of company. Josh seemed as distrusting of her mother's answer as Elaan. Perhaps she should have said something. "I don't know if she knows more than she's letting on or not. Whatever she knows, it may not matter. It's just a guess on her part, until she goes over the data. Let's just let her do that."

Josh raked his hands down the sides of his jeans and sighed. "OK. Fair enough."

"We still may not know," she admitted, as she looked toward the window with the drawn curtain. "She needs more time."

Elaan took in a breath and took in the room. It was fairly sparse. Wood floors, a set of bunk beds just beyond the door, and a dresser on the opposite side. No mirror anywhere in the room, and nothing else, either. No posters, no paintings, no personal touches at all. Mark Dayton must not have wanted to decorate it at all. Complete functionality with no personality.

Elaan lowered her head and sat on the bottom bunk. "God, I'm tired, Josh."

He sat down next to her, their weight making the bedsprings groan. "Yeah, me, too," he admitted, wrapping his arm around her. "I feel like we've spent so much energy just getting here, that there's nothing left."

She nodded. There was nothing left but questions. Always more questions. Elaan lay her head on Josh's shoulder and closed her eyes. She wanted nothing more than to rest.

"Careful," Josh whispered in her ear. "Or you'll fall asleep right here."

"I don't care," Elaan whispered back, feeling comfy in Josh's arms. "I like falling asleep this way."

***

Elaan was awakened by a hand shaking her gently. She heard her mother say her name and opened her eyes, startled. She'd thought she was at home in her bed. Her real bed in her real house, the one she'd grown up in. She'd expected to see her mother, dark skin, pearly white smile, shoulder-length tresses, standing over her. Only her mother's hair was shorn, there was no smile, and the woman was kneeling next to her. And they weren't home. They weren't in her room. There was no sun streaming in, no skylight, and no four-poster bed. Instead it was a bunk, and she was under a — she turned to look — she was under a red fleece blanket unlike any she had at home.

And of course her life came flooding back to her, and she sat up. The world was cold, harsh, and scary again. Not like the dream, where she'd been home having dinner with her parents and Lijah and Josh. A dinner where her mother had smiled and said how much she liked Josh. A dinner where Lijah had said she and Josh were a cute couple.

"You alright, honey?" her mother asked, her eyes watching Elaan closely, searching for signs of distress.

Elaan nodded. She was in Josh's bed, she realized. In his bunk. Her mother didn't seem upset though. The mother in her dream, as much as she liked Josh, would not have been OK finding her daughter in a boy's bed. "Where's Josh?" Elaan asked.

"Taking a shower," her mother said, then turned toward the open doorway. "It's almost time for dinner, so I suggested he shower beforehand, if he wanted to. Told him I'd wake you so he could have his room back."

Elaan nodded. "Yeah, we were talking, and I fell asleep."

She watched her a little more intently, and then said, "That's what he told me, when he asked me if I had an extra blanket. Said you were so tired you'd fallen asleep mid-conversation."

Her mother seemed a tad skeptical, but Elaan ignored it. "Well, it was nice of him to let me stay where I was instead of waking me up."

Shonda shrugged and gave a curt "yeah."

Elaan wasn't sure why, but she got the feeling her mother disliked Josh. "Mom," she said, deciding to just flat-out ask. "You like Josh, don't you? I mean, he's been nothing but helpful to me."

Shonda took a deep breath, and said softly, "Josh seems very nice, but he reminds me a little too much of his father."

Her mother stood and walked toward the door, motioning Elaan to follow. Elaan swept aside the blanket and stood. That was the oddest and most unexpected statement her mother could have said. Cognizant that Josh was across the hall with the shower water running, Elaan spoke in a low voice. "He's nothing like Kingston Wells, Mom," she said.

"Kingston is a class-one asshole."

Shonda frowned and said, "Language, please."

Elaan frowned in response. *Seriously, she lobs a grenade like that and then gets upset about language?* "Fine, he's not a nice man."

Shonda nodded. "Very true," she agreed. "But you don't get to be in his position without being nice to some people along the way. And that" — she pointed her finger across the hall at the closed bathroom door — "reminds me of Kingston Wells when he's acting nice. But it's just an act, because Kingston Wells is a class-one asshole."

Shonda crossed the hall and knocked on that door. "Josh, food will be ready in about ten minutes, and I've woken Elaan, so you've got your room all to yourself, now."

Josh called out to her, "Thanks, Mrs. Woodson," and her mother walked away.

Elaan stood there staring at the door. Josh like his father? There was no way. Was there?

28

Dinner was tasty. It had been a long time since Elaan had eaten a home-cooked meal. Her mother had been able to do a lot with very little. Some beans, some vegetables, some spices, and rice. Apparently, there was a garden out back, but it was done for the year due to the weather. Her mother had frozen most of the growth to last them through the winter. She'd hinted that the veggies would have to be rationed, to avoid running through their food stores too quickly.

It was just another reminder of how desolate their situation was. They had only themselves to rely on.

Elaan tried to remain cheery throughout dinner. Despite comparing Josh to his father, her mother was quite chatty and overly solicitous with Josh. It made Elaan wonder if this was a "keep your friends close and your enemies closer" situation. Her mother didn't seem like the conniving type. Well, the mother she thought she knew wasn't conniving. This mother had faked her death, lied to her children, and lived under the radar for several months. Maybe this Shonda was that type.

After dinner, they all pitched in cleaning up, and then Shonda went to the computer to examine the data her father had sent. She suggested Amadu show them his stereo fix and play some music.

Elaan was trying to keep an open mind toward Amadu. She could ostensibly still see that he was an attractive guy, but she'd taken an immediate dislike to him once she thought her mother was sleeping with him. However, her mother said she wasn't, and Amadu hadn't been particularly affectionate in the few interactions she'd seen. Elaan decided to try to view Amadu the way she'd viewed her mother's teaching assistants, who occasionally came over to the house: as just part of the package of having a mom who's a professor. Amadu was part of the package of Mom in a world turned upside down.

Amadu was friendly enough. He showed Elaan and Josh the stereo and the CDs that went along with it. A lot of the CDs were actual albums, but a half dozen were burned CDs with hand-scrawled labels. Those had newer songs on them, ones Elaan was more inclined to listen to. "Want to Whip and Nae Nae?" she asked Josh with a grin.

"What if I just want to Nae Nae?" he responded, grinning back at them.

"Personally, I like to Superman," Amadu added, in his thick Ghanaian accent. Elaan laughed at his joke. She could see why her mother liked Amadu. He was quiet and contemplative, yet still fun, popping into the conversation at exactly the right moment with something humorous. Something that showed he was familiar with the Silento song, as it featured several dance names, including the Whip, the Nae Nae, the Bop, and the Superman.

Elaan glanced at Josh. He wasn't smiling. Apparently, he didn't find Amadu's sentiment remotely amusing.

"So, how did you come to be staying here?" Josh

asked.

"I was living nearby and ran into Shonda. We had some trouble with looters at my place, and we thought it best to team up. She invited me to stay here, and given how lonely it is trying to survive by yourself, I jumped at the invitation."

Elaan nodded. "Mom said you're a student at one of the universities here."

"U of I," he replied. "The Urbana/Champaign campus."

"And you were studying engineering, but it took you a month to fix the stereo?" Josh asked.

Whoa! That was a Kingston Wells thing to say. Elaan stared at Josh. Her mother couldn't be right, could she?

"Chemical engineering student," Amadu said. He smiled when he spoke, but his eyes flashed anger. "So, yes, it took me longer than I would have liked. But I did have to hunt for a few parts from other appliances around the house."

Elaan wanted to ease the tension, so she quickly popped in the homemade CD, and the first chords of Silento's song beckoning people to Whip and Nae Nae began to play.

"I've had a long day," Amadu said loud enough to be heard over the music. "I'm going to bed. Goodnight, Elaan," he said, smiling at her. He simply turned and nodded to Josh.

Elaan had an urge to tell Amadu he needn't run off, but Josh was being a bit of a jerk, so it was probably for the best. She wasn't sure why he was in such a bad mood, but she didn't want to delve deeply right now. There was music. Not bad music. She and Josh listened to a few songs. Elaan even danced a little, just to feel like life was a little bit normal. She convinced Josh to join her for a couple of songs, but then his expression soured, and he sat down. At a lull between songs, she said, "Hey, can I talk to you?"

He nodded and they left the living room and went back to Josh's room. Given the room's limited furniture, Elaan headed to the only seating option available: the bunk bed. Josh closed the bedroom door and then joined her on the lower bunk.

"What's up?" he asked.

She took in a short breath and tried to calm her demeanor. "What's going on with you?" She hoped not to sound judgmental, but wanted and answer.

He shrugged, smiled, and said, "Nothing, I'm fine."

She shook her head. "You basically accused Amadu of being some kind of liar or charlatan, which is so not cool. I admit I wasn't that keen on him when we arrived, but he's been nothing but nice to us."

He dipped his head in apology. "I'm sorry," he said. "I'll apologize to him in the morning. I'm just in...I don't know. I just feel a little out of place, and I took it out on him. I won't do it again."

She put a hand on Josh's shoulder. "Out of place?" she asked, unsure what he meant.

Josh took a deep breath. "It's been a long journey, and the whole time our goal was to get here. That was what we were focused on. I just thought we'd have peace or happiness or just information, when we got here. But, we don't have any of that. Your mother's as clueless about what happened as we are. And I don't know what we're going to do now. I mean, in the compound, our fathers were trying to find a vaccine, something to make people better. We were waiting for that. Once we left, we were trying to find safety, away from the government. What is there now that we're here? Is this really safety? And how long can we hole up here? And Amadu stares at me, watches me. I feel like he doesn't trust me. And your mother doesn't like me at all. I'm feeling just a little bit lost, and I took it out on Amadu. I shouldn't have. I'm sorry."

Elaan couldn't help feeling awed. What Josh said to her was amazingly perceptive and accurate. They were here, but now what? Besides eating home-cooked meals, what were they supposed to do? Were they safe? And how had he known? How had he figured out that her mother didn't like him?

"Why do you think my mom doesn't like you?"

"It's the way she talks to me. Very chatty, very friendly, sorta, but something about it feels off, like she's testing me, trying to figure out who I am. Like she doesn't believe the truth of what I'm telling her. It's like she plans to keep asking me questions until I slip up. It's the kind of thing my mother would do."

The implication was there. "The kind of thing your mother would do as a spy?"

"As a human being who wanted knowledge, but yes, also as a spy. There are general techniques to use when talking to people to gain their trust. Certain things you insert into conversation, a general friendliness you need to muster, but you also can just be genuine. People like genuineness."

Elaan realized her mouth was hanging open. "How do you know all this?"

"Do you know what percentage of the population has an eidetic memory?"

Elaan shook her head.

"Two percent," he said. "Do you think that a spy

with a kid who's eidetic doesn't consider what that kid could do if he were a spy?"

"I don't know," she said. "I never really thought about it."

He laughed. "Well, maybe it wasn't a desire to see me as a spy. Perhaps it was a simple desire to make sure that if things got weird, if we had to change identities or travel someplace that I would always fit in. Even before she told me what she did, she always had advice on reading people, on adapting to situations, on ways to tell if people were lying, on ways to fit in quickly in a new situation. It was easy enough stuff to learn, and she'd practice with me, coach me. She was good at it, better than me or my father. She used to tell my dad ways to get along better, but he has a bit of a stubborn streak, so he wouldn't listen. And, on some level, I think he liked being the guy to buck against the norm. He liked being different. But, I know when people are testing me and your mother is."

Elaan wasn't sure what to say to that. He'd probably assessed her mother correctly. Shonda had admitted she wasn't keen on Josh, so it wasn't a stretch to think she was testing him. "She's my mom," Elaan said. "We've been traveling alone for days. I think she just wants to make sure you're as nice as I think you are." She glanced down at her lap, debating whether to say the next part, but then chose to go ahead. "Plus, she knows your father, and I don't think she liked him that much. She probably just wants to make sure you're more like your mother than your father."

He sighed, nodded. "Maybe," he said.

Elaan leaned her head on Josh's shoulder. He

wrapped an arm around her, and they sat like that for a while. It was nice, until an errant thought occurred to Elaan. She pulled away from Josh and turned to look at him in a new light.

"What is it?" he asked.

She hesitated a moment, but then decided to come out with it. "I guess I always thought you were just naturally good with people, naturally a nice guy. But now, with what you just told me, I wonder, are you just good at acting nice?"

Josh stroked her cheek. "Hey," he said. "I am a nice guy."

Elaan stared into his green eyes, wanting nothing more than to believe.

"I have never pretended with you. I am a nice guy, OK." He leaned forward and kissed her, his lips soft and warm. Her tummy fluttered and her toes curled when he kissed her. That still felt so real.

He pulled back and smiled. "I have always been real with you," he said. "It's the thing I've liked most about you since we met. You don't want lies and pretend. You want real. You see real. You know when someone is faking. Maybe that's why I agreed to go along with Lijah when he asked me not to see you. I knew inevitably that we'd end up here. Where you found out that I hadn't told you everything, even though I told you everything I could at the time."

"And have you told me everything now?"

Josh shook his head, half laughed. "Nope," he said. "There's more. But not much more. I don't know that you'll care. It just has to do with what my father packed me."

"Besides the gun?"

He laughed. "Yes, besides that. And I wasn't trying

to hide that from you. I just didn't think a lot about it. It was only for use in a dire emergency. It was if I needed it. Well, he also passed me one other thing: a satellite phone with GPS."

Elaan crinkled her brows. "I don't understand. How will that help?"

"Well, presuming the person on the other end answers, it could offer me help. I mean, the satellite's floating in space, and it should work for relaying signals."

Elaan nodded but wasn't sure where Josh was going with this. "Who would you call?"

"Depends. I could call my dad, presuming things got better. Presuming the world got fixed. If not, there's someone at the CIA. A friend of my mom's. He thinks that person would help me, if I needed it, and if he could."

"Who is he?"

He raised an eyebrow and pursed his lips. He watched her a minute and finally said, "His name is Linc, but I'm not sure that helps you much."

"Link, like a chain-link fence?"

"Like Honest Abe. Short for Lincoln."

"Oh," she said as the explanation dawned on her. "Who is he?"

"Just a friend of my mom's. Someone who can help, if he's still alive."

Elaan gazed toward the door. "Do you think he is?"

Josh gave an immediate nod. "He was in an SPU, too, one in New York, so probably." He turned back and looked at the closed door to his room. "Um, I trust you completely, and I don't care that you know these things, but I'd appreciate it if you kept this between us. It's not something everyone needs to know."

Elaan nodded. While she didn't like secrets, this wasn't hers to tell, nor was it really anyone else's business. Josh leaned in and kissed her. She did believe him, did believe that he was a nice guy. Her mother was wrong about Josh being like Kingston. His hands slid along the side of her shirt, his fingers caressing the skin of her spine. His kiss had turned fierce and unrelenting. He seemed to desperately need his kisses returned, so she did. She kissed him back, her hands sliding her fingers beneath his shirt and up his warm back. His fingers grazed her bare skin, and it was like pure ecstasy. He leaned her back onto the bed, kissing her neck.

A knock on the door startled them both. Josh had just pulled away from her when the door opened and her mother peeked in.

Josh had turned beet red, and Elaan was pretty sure she could brighten any room just by her embarrassed glow. Her wide-eyed mother disappeared out the door. Elaan was standing up and straightening her shirt, when she heard her mother call from the other side of the door. "Elaan, I wanted to talk to you."

"OK, Mom," she called back. "One second."

Guilt flashed across her face. "Sorry," she whispered as she trundled out the bedroom door to find her mother in the hall, standing outside the door to their room. Shonda opened the door to go in and Elaan followed.

Once they were in, Elaan turned to her mother. She thought she should say something to her mother but couldn't think of what. "I can explain" seemed to be a thing to say, yet, she couldn't. Well, she could, but she didn't want to explain. Saying, "It's not what it looked like" also crossed her mind. But that wasn't true, either. It was exactly what it looked like. Also a good reason not to try to explain.

"Elaan," Shonda said, her voice calm and resolute. "I am aware that you and Josh have been thrown into a very adult situation, and that you have traveled by yourselves to get here and may have done things together out there that you wanted to do."

She wanted to disagree with her mother. She opened her mouth to say something, but she wasn't sure what. Her mother hadn't actually asked her do anything or refrain from doing anything. So, she closed her mouth.

"But you're not out on the road anymore. You're here with me, and I'd appreciate it if you would treat this place the way you treated our home. If you'd act in ways you considered appropriate when we all lived at home as a family."

Elaan stared at her mother, wondering exactly what she was saying. "This isn't home. You're living here with Amadu."

Her mother sighed. "Alright," she said. "Fair point. It's not home. And we're not in that world. I can't pretend we are and make you behave like the seventeen-year-old daughter who lived there, the one who was not allowed to have boys in her bedroom."

Well technically, she'd been in Josh's bedroom. He hadn't been in hers, but Elaan thought raising that point at the moment was unwise. Shonda reached out and took her daughter's hand. "I know you were hurt by what I did. And I am truly sorry about that. What I want now, and I know it will take time, is for you to trust me again. And to talk to me, again. And to feel safe here."

Shonda glanced at the closed door and bit her lip before turning back to her daughter. "I can see Josh means a lot to you. Because you're a good judge of character, I'm going to trust in you, that you've pegged him right, and not make any more assumptions about him based on his father."

Elaan smiled. That was good of her.

"What I'd like you to do is to give me the benefit

of the doubt, and be respectful, remembering that as the mother of a seventeen-year-old daughter who is beautiful, smart, and resourceful, I'm going to have concerns about any guys she's with. It just means I'm your mother and I love you. It doesn't mean I'm trying to hurt you or bother you."

Elaan nodded. "I know."

Shonda sighed and released her. "Good."

"So, does that conclude what you wanted to talk to me about?"

Shonda shook her head. "Well, not really," she said, with a laugh. "I'd really just been heading to bed. I'd expected to find you in our room, and when I didn't, I stopped in to tell you I was calling it a night."

Elaan rolled her eyes. "Well, now I know."

Her mother gave her a hint of side eye. "Yes, you do," she said. "But you should probably call it a night too."

Elaan checked her watch. It was after eleven and she was tired. Since her mother had promised to keep an open mind about Josh, she figured it best to agree and go to bed. She just needed to tell Josh goodnight, first. She was about to leave, when she remembered what her mother had been doing before talking to her. "Mom," she said. "Did you figure out what Dad was trying to tell you on the drive?"

Her mother shook her head. "Not entirely," she said. "I think I know where he's going with this, but I'd really like to see your brother's drive. Plus, it's late and I think I'd evaluate things better after a little sleep."

* * *

Elaan awoke the next morning to find her mother

gone from their room. She got up, stretched her legs, wearing one of her mother's nightgowns.

Elaan left the room and found her mother staring at the computer. She walked over to her, put a hand on her shoulder. "You making any headway?"

Her mother shook her head. "No more than last night," she said. She smiled at her. "Would you like some coffee?"

Elaan stared at her. "You have coffee?"

Shonda laughed. "I know," she said. "It's completely impractical, but I was depressed after I left…. left everyone behind, my family. I wanted coffee. It's my one vice, so I went to Sam's Club after I got here, and I bought massive quantities of coffee. It was completely impractical and I should have bought more important supplies, but I just wanted one thing I could have in my life to make me happy, even if it was stupid."

Elaan couldn't help but grin. That was so like her mother. It was the essence of her, on some level. She always said life was hard, that life might not treat you fair, but you had to have a good attitude, and you had to find one bright spot in your life. Even though the whole world was falling apart, Shonda was going to wake up with her morning cup of coffee, come hell or high water.

Elaan was actually glad for it. She liked coffee. When Elaan was fourteen, her mother had finally given up on saying it would stunt her growth. Now, Elaan liked hers with cream and sugar, whereas Shonda drank hers black. Elaan liked the fresh smell of it, and the way you could feel it perk you right up in the morning.

"You have any sugar?"

Shonda shook her head. "Sorry, babe. But I do have milk."

Elaan shrugged. Coffee without sugar. Blech. "I'll pass."

Shonda nodded and headed over to the kitchen. Elaan followed and watched as her mother made a pot of coffee. "What are you going to do if the power stops?"

"I've got filters," Shonda said. "And we have a fireplace. Probably just heat the water over the fire and pour it over the coffee."

Elaan shook her head. "The apocalypse is upon us, but Mom still has coffee," she said with a laugh. "I meant, in general, if there's no power, will this still be a good place to stay?"

"Oh," her mother said. "Yeah. It should be fine. It's got a fireplace for heat. I think that's the main concern as it gets colder." Shonda gazed at the coffee pot and sighed. "I guess this is the apocalypse, isn't it?"

Elaan stopped smiling. "I was sorta kidding, but I know things are bad with the virus. I know this isn't what life is supposed to be like, but surely you don't think it's as bad as all that?"

Shonda was watching the coffee drip from the filter into the pot. "I think that whatever happened a month ago caused a lot of people to die, and I'm beginning to wonder if what we don't know can really, really hurt us."

Elaan watched her mother closely, hoping for some sign that this wasn't as serious as it sounded. There was no such indication. "How can we find out? We don't know what happened, and no one's talking."

Her mother grabbed a cup and set it on the counter. "I think Amadu and I might have to venture out, try to get to town, see if someone will talk to us."

Elaan's eyes widened. "No," she said. "Last time you went to town, you brought back bandits."

"We need to figure it out," she said. "I feel like we've done all we can here at the house. There's nothing more for me to figure out with what I have." She stared into the coffee mug and bit her lower lip. "I wish your father were here, or Lijah. He knew a little bit about the research. I just wish I knew where he was."

A wave of guilt and self-disgust washed over her. It was her fault Lijah wasn't here with them. "I'm sorry, Mom. I wish I could've convinced him to come."

Shonda patted Elaan's shoulder and shook her head. "You did the right thing and Lijah did the right thing. Don't feel guilty. I'm just a mother who's worried about my son. I don't blame you for anything. It's the government that's caused the problem, trying to take you. Trying to experiment on you. Your father was right to get you out."

They'd gotten out, but now what? What were they supposed to do? Josh's words from the other night reverberated through her mind. She heard footsteps, and turned to see Josh entering the kitchen.

"Is that coffee?" he asked, looking cheerful and neat. He didn't even have bed head. She wondered if he'd groomed himself before coming out. He must've. He hadn't looked that way when they woke up together these past few days. She missed waking up with him, she realized.

"Yep," Shonda said. "Would you like a cup? Be

forewarned. I have no sugar."

"I like it black," Josh said. Shonda nodded, grabbed a mug from the cabinet, and poured Josh a cup.

Josh took a sip, and smiled. "This is good. Hadn't realized how much I missed it."

Shonda nodded. "Yeah, it's my one indulgence here."

"Is Amadu awake?" Josh asked.

Shonda nodded. "Yeah, he went out fishing. They bite early, and I think he wanted to try to catch a few, since there are more of us."

Josh nodded, as if this made sense. It did. He stood there, sipping his coffee, leaning against the wall, while Elaan stood near her mother at the countertop. There was silence, a slightly uncomfortable one. Elaan decided to break the peace. She filled Josh in on what her mother had told her.

Josh finished off his coffee, and set the mug down on the nearby counter. "Thanks for the coffee, Mrs. Woodson. Is it alright if I go for a walk?"

Shonda nodded. "Sure," she said. "You're not a prisoner here. You can come and go as you please."

Josh nodded to Shonda, gave Elaan a pat on the hand, then walked off, heading down the stairs and presumably outside.

After they heard the thud of a door closing downstairs, Shonda spoke. "He seems disillusioned."

Elaan nodded. "Yeah, it's hard not to be, with the world the way it is."

Shonda took Josh's coffee mug to the sink and then refilled her own cup. "Honey, I spent a lot of time here wondering what I did to deserve this, and the answer is nothing. Sometimes the world is just a hard place. We have to take what joy we can from what we have. Some days it's something small like coffee. On other days, it's something big, like your daughter coming back to you. Josh will find his thing."

Josh. Yeah, maybe Josh would. "But what about me?" Elaan asked.

"You've always had your thing, and you have it still, even now."

Elaan raised an eyebrow.

"You need to know the truth. Even now, with everything that's going on, your focus is on why this happened, what the data means, why we're here. And once you know, you'll find something else you want to know the truth about. That's the thing about the world, baby. It's full of secrets, and I think you'll always be driven because there will always be something to ferret out."

30

They'd been in Dahinda for a week, and things had taken on a natural rhythm. Josh had apologized to Amadu, and the two seemed to get along well enough that they went fishing together. Some days they caught stuff. Other days, they didn't.

Elaan had gotten to know Amadu a bit, and he seemed like a genuinely nice guy. She could see why her mother liked him. He was easy to get along with and unobtrusive. She'd also learned he was gay, an interesting tidbit in light of Lijah. Her mother had said nothing was going on between her and Amadu, but Elaan wondered if she was using him. Not in a sexual way, of course, but in the way Lee had used her the other day. Lee had said Elaan reminded him of his daughter. That by helping Elaan, it was like he was paying it forward for Natalie. She wondered if her mother had made the same conscious — or even, unconscious — choice. Had she glommed onto Amadu to make up for the rift between her and her son?

On the bright side, Josh had been in better spirits, and her mother seemed to be taking a liking to him. It probably helped that they all had something tangible to plan and do. They'd decided as a group, they needed more information to help them figure out what Elaan's father was trying to tell them.

The only way to get more information was to go out and find it. The tentative plan was for Josh and Amadu to take the bike into town and see what they could learn while they bought supplies.

They'd considered all going, but Shonda didn't want everyone to leave the house in case Lijah came. Shonda was sure he'd turn up. She'd suggested she and Elaan stay while Josh and Amadu made the trek. Josh thought that was best since it seemed unlikely anyone would cause them trouble at the house. The doors were locked, and there were weapons. For a man of God, Dayton had a lot of firepower. There were at least six handguns, three rifles, and a shotgun. Josh had given her a rudimentary lesson in how to use a couple of the automatic weapons, which appeared to be a misnomer. There was a lot more to a gun than point and shoot. You had to know whether the gun had a safety on and whether there was a bullet loaded in the chamber. More complicated than she'd expected. Though, once those things were accomplished, it was apparently quite easy. Elaan hadn't gotten a lot of practice because they wanted to conserve ammunition. Though, she thought she had the basics.

Josh and Amadu had headed down to the lake to fish this morning, so it was just Shonda and Elaan. Things had gotten easier between them. In part, it was just nice to have her mother back. As much as she'd been angry about the lies, she was also glad to be with her mom. And her mother was being motherly. She made meals. She'd ask about life in the compound. She even showed her the data on the drive, even though Elaan didn't understand half of it. Having her mother with her was nice. And of course, it had helped tremendously that her mother had warmed to Josh.

Elaan peered out the back windows at the trees. This was a nice little community. And it still was livable, even after all the disease. "I wonder why some communities have power, while other seem to be out. And, I really wish we had the Internet. I want to know what's going on other places."

Her mother was doing pushups. This was Shonda's morning routine. She said it was important to be physically fit because you never knew when you'd have to up and leave or what kind of rigors might be necessary. Though, her mother was preaching to the choir. Elaan had walked and biked two hundred miles. She knew the body had to be ready. She preferred to exercise outside, running the path between the house and the lake. It was a little monotonous, but after spending so much time underground, she liked being outside. She liked feeling the cool air on her face, seeing birds, bees, spiders, trees, leaves. She'd exercise for an hour outside then come in, on most days. Sometimes, she and Josh would go for a short walk down to the lake, but her mother had told her not to venture too far from the house, lest they bring unwanted attention to themselves.

"Mom," Elaan said, as her mother switched to sit-ups. "Do you think there are people out there who would attack the house, who would watch and wait for us to go, or Josh and Amadu to go?"

Shonda pulled up, and stopped. "Elaan, I think the possibility is slim, but given what happened to me and Amadu, we can't discount it. But don't worry, we're prepared if it happens."

Maybe Shonda was prepared, but Elaan wasn't. Despite Josh showing her how to use the guns, she didn't feel particularly confident with them in her hands. Perhaps that was because she'd only been holding a gun around people she cared about, and the prospect of accidentally shooting someone she loved weighed heavily on her.

"Hey," her mother was saying, and Elaan was startled to see her mother standing right in front of her. She'd been so deep in thought, she hadn't even seen her mother end her workout and walk over.

"Hey," she said back.

Shonda squatted in front of her daughter. "Listen," she said. "I know you're worried, but you have to remember, we're strong women."

Elaan wanted to scoff. She remembered Willie on the train. She remembered how he'd looked at her, what he'd asked of her, and how she'd cringed away from him. How she'd hidden behind Josh and Lijah. How she had done exactly nothing strong in that situation. All she did was be scared and let her brother sacrifice himself for her. "I think you're thinking of you, Mom. You're strong."

Shonda put a hand on Elaan's knee. "Honey, you think because you let Lijah handle the situation on the train that you're not strong," she said, the words hitting home.

Elaan sometimes wondered if her mother was a mind reader, the way she seemed to delve right into her thoughts. Elaan nodded.

"Being strong is not just lifting a hundred-pound weight and chucking it across a field. Being strong is knowing your own strengths and weaknesses and using your strengths to your advantage. Being strong is assessing a situation, and understanding who can handle it best. Being strong is leaving even when you want to stay. You didn't want to leave Lijah, but you were strong enough to know that it was for the best and that he could take care of himself. Then, you took care of yourself and made it all the way here. You walked and biked across two states to get here, and you didn't let insects and lack of shelter stop you. You were a woman on a mission, and you got here because you're strong."

Elaan smiled at her mother. Shonda knew how to spin. "You're the black Pollyanna, Mom."

"Ain't nothing wrong with Pollyanna," Shonda said. "She gets it done. Because she's not a bully, people act like she's not strong, but she was a tough cookie. If they were updating the movie, she'd be tough as nails, and you'd see internet memes describing her as a total BAMF."

Elaan laughed out loud. "Mom, what is a BAMF?"

Shonda frowned. "I thought I was totally up on all the cool lingo, but maybe that's just cool among us geeks. I saw a picture of Nichelle Nichols with a BAMF tag right before all this started."

Elaan wasn't sure who Nichelle Nichols was, but she didn't want to ask and have her mother go into a lengthy discussion of this person.

Shonda stood up and shook her head. "My greatest failure as a parent was not introducing you to *Star Trek* at a young age. I just thought it would trickle down since Lijah and I watched it."

It hadn't. "You let me believe you were dead and you consider your greatest parenting failure not introducing me to *Star Trek*?"

Shonda gave her a look that said cut-it-out-Miss-

Smarty-Pants. "OK, perhaps that wasn't my greatest failure, but surely it's the one that's hindering our conversation right now. Nichelle Nichols, since you have no idea who she is, she was the original Lieutenant Uhura in *Star Trek*. And she is, by all accounts, a BAMF, or a bad ass mother — um well, you get the gist."

"Language, Mom," Elaan teased.

Her mother nodded. "Duly noted. Just remember, the people who have survived in the world of the virus, the people who have endured what you endured to get here, those people are all BAMFs. That means you and that means me. It means Amadu, and it means Josh. We've got the grit that will keep us surviving. So, if you are ever feeling doubtful, remember what you've survived, and remember who you are. I'm your mother and I wouldn't lie."

Elaan gave her a look to remind her mother she'd already lied quite a bit.

"OK, I did lie about being dead. But I wouldn't lie about this. You're a BAMF."

"As BAMF as Nichelle?" Elaan asked.

"All that and more, baby." Shonda smiled. "You don't even need a phaser."

With that Shonda winked, and said she was going to grab a quick shower before the guys got back.

Elaan sat back in her chair and closed her eyes. She wasn't convinced her mother was right. She didn't feel strong, though she did think it would be cool to be a BAMF. She took a deep breath and listened, hearing the soft strains of water running through the pipes as her mother showered. If she closed her eyes, this could be just like being at home. Her real home. Her sitting in a chair, her mother in the other room taking a shower. All they needed was Lijah playing on his Xbox and her father in his study reviewing some scientific paper he was set to publish.

That was when she heard the noise, the heavy thuds of someone knocking on the door. Then it stopped. She opened her eyes, and looked toward the front door. The shades were drawn. She wondered for a moment if she'd imagined the knocking. The air was silent, and the door was still. Then the pounding began again, persistent, angry.

BAMF she was not, Elaan decided. Her mother was still in the shower. She glanced at the front door, then back toward the kitchen, where Josh had set one of the handguns on the table. BAMF, she told herself. She started toward the kitchen to grab the gun. The person knocking spoke. "Hello? Anyone home."

"Lijah," Elaan said, forgetting all thoughts of guns. She ran to the door and fumbled with the locks. "Lijah," she called out as she flung open the door.

31

Lijah watched Elaan's face crumple when she opened the door. It was as if she'd expected to see someone else. Lijah knew his journey had been long and he'd had a rough few nights, but he hadn't expected his sister to recoil at the sight of him.

She seemed to recover from her initial shock, grabbing his free hand and pulling him toward her. "Come in, quickly," she said, peeking behind him, then closing the door and locking it.

He walked in and dropped his backpack on the floor, looking around. The house seemed nice and comfy. Better than any place he'd stayed along his journey. And it seemed to have… running water. He was sure he could hear water. And electricity? Maybe. There were no lights on, but he thought he heard the electronic hum of something, a refrigerator or an air conditioner maybe. Though, it was pretty cool today, so they shouldn't need air conditioning?

He was about to ask where Josh was, when Elaan wrapped her arms around him, squeezing him tight. "Lijah," she said, her voice muffled by his shirt. "I'm so glad. I've been so worried. I thought you were dead. I thought Willie'd gotten the upper hand." She was murmuring something else, but her words were lost as she squeezed him tighter.

He hugged her back, and said, "I'm fine." He'd

almost not come, but this, her reaction, was the reason he had changed his mind. He knew she'd be worried. And she had been. He patted her back and pulled away. He was tired. It had been an exhausting journey. He pulled away from her and spotted the sofa. "Can we sit?"

Her expression turned to slight embarrassment at not having realized his fatigue. "Yes," she said, leading him toward the sofa. "I should have offered you a seat first thing."

When they got to the sofa, he plopped down, thankful for the soft padding. It was the nicest — well, actually, only — furniture he'd had the pleasure of using since he'd left the cabin.

Elaan was staring at him with sorrow in her eyes. "Lijah, I can't lie," she said. "You look awful. Are you alright? Did you want something to eat or drink?"

He closed his eyes. Did he? "Some water would be good," he said, opening his eyes long enough to see her hurry away to get his drink. He closed his eyes again, just wanting to rest.

"Lijah," he heard her say, and lifted his gaze in time to see Elaan handing him a glass of water. He took it, gulped it down, and set the cup aside. The cool water was refreshing.

He closed his eyes again, still just wanting to rest. He knew Elaan was interested in talking, in finding out what had happened to him. But he wasn't ready to talk. He wanted to be someplace nice and forget the world he'd just come from. He felt a hand on his own and opened his eyes to see Elaan staring with wide eyes and a creased brow. "Lijah, you're scaring me. What happened to you out there?"

Lijah breathed out, steeling himself against the

memories. What had happened out there? He didn't want to talk about it. "Is she here?"

Elaan frowned, as if disappointed he hadn't answered her question. "Yeah, she's here. She's been living here with an immune engineering student."

Lijah raised an eyebrow. "An engineering student?" he asked. "A guy?"

Elaan nodded. "His name is Amadu," she said. "He's originally from Ghana, and he's pretty nice."

He scoffed. His mother took the cake. The world was disintegrating, and she decided to go cougar with a college student. He rubbed his temples. "So Mom's been mourning herself by having a Netflix and Chill moment, sans the Netflix?"

Elaan rolled her eyes. "No, it's not like that," she said. "I see why you thought it. I thought the same thing you did when I got here. But it's not true. For one, Mom says she's in love with Dad and she's never been unfaithful."

Like that was supposed to mean something. God, he hated that she still believed every word their mother said.

"Second," Elaan said louder, "Even if that were a lie, she's not lying about Amadu. I've seen them together. There's nothing going on there. Plus, he's not interested in women."

Lijah raised a brow. His heart double thumped in his chest. Gay. She picked up a young gay refugee to live with. A college student, someone around his age, a guy, a gay guy. He wondered briefly if she was drawn to this guy because she yearned for the son she'd left behind. He shook his head. He didn't want to be sucked into anything involving her, or her need to make up for her wrongs.

"Elijah?" he heard his mother cry out, stunned. He turned to see her running toward him. She looked different; her hair was shorter, and she was thinner, but she seemed more toned, less soft than he remembered. In a few seconds, she was kneeling before him, examining his face, touching the scar on his forehead. "Son," she whispered, her expression full of concern. "What happened to you?"

He couldn't get away from that question. No matter how much he deflected. No matter how much he tried to ignore it, they kept coming back to that. And wasn't that why he'd decided to come in the first place? To tell them what had happened, what he'd learned of the outside world, of what had happened a month ago. He supposed he'd have to tell them. There seemed to be no getting around it.

32

L ijah suggested his mother and sister sit down. "It's a long story," he said.

"Do you want something to eat or drink, first?" Shonda asked. "You look hungry."

He'd already had something to drink, and he wasn't ready to talk. So, it was probably best to eat. He was, in fact, hungry. He'd eaten some berries and even had gotten lucky enough a couple of days ago to stumble across an apple tree. It was sustenance, but apples were certainly not what people dreamed about eating. Not for breakfast, lunch, and dinner. "I am hungry," he said. "What do you have?"

Shonda offered leftover fish from yesterday, some lentils, even a cup of coffee.

"How about all three," he said.

His mother smiled at him. "Just give me two minutes to heat it up." She headed toward the kitchen and began taking out the leftovers.

Elaan was sitting in her chair, tapping her feet. Impatient as ever. Yearning for the truth, still. He missed her. As annoying as she was, you could always tell where you stood with her. Right now, she didn't want to wait for him to eat, but she knew she should, so she let out all her anxiousness through foot tapping. Only, it was going to drive him mad to watch her so wound up. He decided to ask her the question he'd been curious about since he'd arrived.

"So," Lijah said. "Where's Josh? Did he leave after he brought you here?" Lijah hoped he had. He didn't want to see Josh and Elaan together.

Elaan shook her head. "No, he and Amadu went into town."

Lijah raised an eyebrow. Out with the gay guy. Was Josh a gay magnet? Did he enjoy standing there looking handsome and having gay guys lust over him, even though he wasn't? No, that was stupid. A stupid thought he'd like to erase. Only, he was still somewhat too obsessed over a guy he couldn't have. It was a bad place to be.

"Do you want me to show you around while Mom gets your lunch?"

Lijah shrugged. He was curious about the house. She stood, and he followed her, taking a mild interest in where he would stay. Anything here was better than where he'd been. He'd tried not to cringe when Elaan told him he'd be sharing a room with Josh. He'd deal with that later. Maybe he could convince his mother to let him switch with Amadu. When they'd finished the tour, his mother had a warm plate with fish, lentils, and a hot mug of coffee on the kitchen table.

He sat down and began to eat. His mother and sister joined him at the table even though they'd already eaten. He scarfed down the food quickly, and when he'd finished, they were both staring as if they didn't know him.

He burped. "Excuse me," he said, then took a sip of coffee. He would've liked some sugar, but the warm drink in and of itself was nice. It felt like liquid gold flowing through his body.

"So," his mother said. There was that word again. She was giving him an opening for him to talk, but he didn't want to talk. He took his spoon and tried to scoop up what remained of the sauce.

"What happened to you, Lijah?" Elaan asked, her desire for answers the one thing that was consistent about her. "How did you get away from Boxcar Willie?"

That was an easier question to answer, sort of. He told the story of escaping from Willie, finding the cabin in the woods, and deciding he wanted to stay there.

Shonda's reaction was stony and cold, her face unchanging while he talked. She liked to be neutral sometimes. He used to like it, used to think it was good that she could appear unfazed by anything you said. But now he wondered if it was just the sign of a cold heart.

"So, why did you leave?" Elaan asked. "If you wanted to stay, if you just wanted to be reclusive, avoid the disease?"

Lijah shrugged, then picked up a single lentil left on his plate and popped it in his mouth. It was good. Good, good food. "There were a lot of reasons. Staying meant I wouldn't know if you made it," he said to Elaan. "Josh had promised me he would get you here, but what if he hadn't? What if you hadn't gotten to Mom? I made sure you got off that train, got away from Willie, tried to make sure you were safe. Staying in the cabin meant I wouldn't know if that were true or not."

Elaan's face took on a bit of color, and she reached out and patted Lijah's hands. "I should have said thank you earlier, Lijah." She looked him right in the eye. "Thank you so much for what you did with Willie, for protecting me."

He waved her off. "I was glad to do it," he said. "You're my baby sister."

He caught a glimpse of Shonda. She was smiling, as if it warmed her heart that her children were embarking on a love fest. Sometimes he wondered if he judged her too harshly, if she were just what she said she was, a woman who loved her children but sometimes made mistakes.

"You left to come here?" Shonda asked.

"Yeah, after four days at the cabin, I decided I needed to know. I'd done a pretty good job of eating off the land. I'd picked berries, and even caught a couple of rabbits in traps. They weren't used to trappers, so it was easy enough. Though, killing and cleaning a rabbit with an old knife isn't the easiest or exacting method. I had more waste than I should have. But I also hadn't dug too deeply into the food I'd brought with me. Elaan had given me the Illinois map, so I just had to figure out where I was and get started."

"Where were you?" Elaan asked.

"Greenville, Illinois," he said. "Not so far from St. Louis, and way further south than I wanted to be. According to the map, it was more than two hundred miles from Dahinda."

"You walked two hundred miles," his mother said, peering down at his worn and tattered sneakers.

"Hitchhiked a little ways," Lijah said. "That's

where I found out what happened."

"What do you mean, you found out what happened?" Shonda said.

Lijah looked at Elaan. "You know how the food supplies stopped a month before we left, how they blamed it on contamination?"

Elaan nodded.

"I'm not sure what happened, but sometime, a couple of months ago, the military got infected as carriers. They started spreading the disease unknowingly."

Elaan shook her head. "How do you know this?"

"I don't know anything for sure. Just what the one guy who picked me up told me. He was traveling north and gave me a fifty-mile ride. I told him I'd been in hiding, away from the disease, but now I was trying to see if any family was left. He told me to watch out for soldiers, that everywhere they went, sickness and death followed. He doesn't know what happened or why. He said there were rumors the government is trying to kill people, or that the government mistakenly turned its soldiers into carriers. Regardless, people fear soldiers. Frankly, they fear anyone associated with the government or establishment."

Lijah slid his spoon across the empty plate, hoping to catch a smidgen more food. He was still hungry. His mother and Elaan were silent, digesting the information. It had taken him a while to comprehend it, too. He wondered if his father and Kingston were responsible. Had their vaccine been used on the soldiers? Had they thought it had been fixed? He searched his plate for a smidge of anything left, but he'd done too good a job. There was only a thin layer of sauce.

"Did you actually see any soldiers?" his mother asked.

He looked up from his plate and shook his head. "No," he said. "But I can tell you that people are scared of something. Beside that guy who gave me a ride, most people stayed away from me. They stayed away from everyone. They're not coming together, like you'd expect people to come together in a crisis. That means they're staying away from people they don't know. This lack of people we're seeing, it's fueled not just by the death, but by a general mistrust. I think Scott was right. The infected soldiers caused a massive uptick in death and fear."

"Who's Scott?" Elaan said.

"Guy who gave me a ride."

"And you trust him?" Shonda asked.

Lijah nodded. "I see no reason not to," he said. "What he said made sense. If there was a sudden uptick in illness, then it would explain concerns over contamination at the SPU. It would explain why supplies stopped, why everything changed so quickly."

He watched as his mother and sister mulled over his words. It was a hard thing to reconcile, but he was sure it was true. He'd thought about it so much, as he'd walked through barren streets and towns, seen so few people, so few things open. The places that were open seemed to be the few ones that had maintained power. He wasn't sure exactly what caused certain places to have power and some not to. Though, he'd seen a few wind farms on the way. Perhaps those power plants had been easier to maintain than some of the other types, such as coal-fired plants, which seem like they'd require more active pursuits to generate power.

"This means we should go," Shonda said.

Lijah looked at his mother and sister. "Go where?" Lijah asked.

"We've been worried," his mother said. "Worried that whatever happened a month ago that was causing the trouble was bad news for your father. Bad news for the people in the compound. I'm beginning to think they cut off the food supplies and have just left them there to rot. I want to talk to him, so we were going to try to head east toward the university. Amadu is familiar with it, and if anyone has access to electronics and internet, it would be that place. It's our best bet to try to contact them. And our best bet to try to show them what I figured out."

Lijah stared at her. "And what did you figure out?"

"I've gone over the data your father sent, and looked at all the experiments, all the reactions, all the data, and I think I know where they went wrong. I think I know how to turn off the carrier gene in the vaccine. So that people who get it won't be turned into carriers with exposure."

Lijah's insides tingled. He closed his eyes, opened them again, wondering if what she was saying could really be true. Could she really crack the vaccine code, even though stronger minds had been working on it for months? "Mom, how can you say that? You haven't even been working on the project."

She nodded. "I know, but your father sent me all the data. He had been sending it to me before we lost our internet, and I'd been looking at it, but it's been almost two months since then. And what I have is just a theory, but one I think will work."

Lijah stared at his mother, not really sure he believed her. "Have you tried out your theory?"

"I don't have anything to conduct experiments with," Shonda said. "That's why we were going to try to get to Champaign. Amadu's familiar with the campus, and if school has actually begun, he's supposed to be enrolled. He'd have access to the labs and the equipment we'd need. Maybe I could get a message to your father."

Lijah nodded. "When did you want to go?"

Shonda turned her head and looked out the rear window, toward the tree-lined rear. "Once the boys come back from town, we can talk about a plan, and hopefully leave in a couple of days. The sooner we leave, the better, I think."

Elaan smiled. "Sounds like a plan to me."

END BOOK TWO

Thank you for reading this book. If you enjoyed it, please tell a friend or leave a review. Word of mouth is an author's best friend and much appreciated. The final book in the Virus series, *Contained*, will be published in early August. If you'd like to be notified of Exposed's release, please join the mailing list at http://www.rjcrayton.com/subscribe.

ABOUT THE AUTHOR

RJ Crayton grew up in Illinois and now lives in the Maryland suburbs of Washington, DC. She is the author of the Life First series of novels, which includes *Life First, Second Life* and *Third Life: Taken*. Prior to writing fiction, Crayton was a journalist, writing for newspapers, including the *Wichita Eagle* and *Kansas City Star*. Crayton also worked for several trade publications, including *Solid Waste Report, Education Technology News*, and *Campus Crime*. Crayton is a monthly contributor to the Indies Unlimited blog. When she's not writing, Crayton spends her time being a ninja mom (stealthy and ultra cool, like moms should be) to her son and daughter. You can find out more about her at http://rjcrayton.com.

RJ Crayton loves connecting with readers. If you talk to her, she'll talk back, so please check her out at the following places:

Website
http://rjcrayton.com

Facebook
https://www.facebook.com/rjcraytonauthor

Twitter
https://twitter.com/RJCrayton

Goodreads
http://www.goodreads.com/author/show/7111348.R_J_Crayton

Pinterest
http://www.pinterest.com/rjcrayton